D1123343

APPLE IN THE MIDDLE

APPLE IN THE MIDDLE

BY DAWN QUIGLEY

Contemporary Voice of Indigenous Peoples Series / Volume 1

First Edition
First Printing

This book is a work of fiction. Names, characters, businesses, places, events, locales, and incidents are either the products of the author's imagination or used in a fictitious manner. Any resemblance to actual persons, living or dead, or actual events is purely coincidental.

Library of Congress Control Number: 2018941180
ISBN: 978-1-946163-07-3

Illustration and cover design by Jamie Hohnadel Trosen
Interior design by Deb Tanner
Author photo by Brooke Wood, www.tadpolephoto.com

The publication of *Apple in the Middle* is made possible by the generous support of donors to the NDSU Press Fund and the NDSU Press Endowment Fund, and other contributors to NDSU Press.

David Bertolini, Director
Suzzanne Kelley, Editor in Chief
Zachary Vietz, Publicist Intern
Marie Wagar, Publishing Intern

Book Team for *Apple in the Middle*
Samantha Kise, Preston Olson, Marie Wagar

Printed in Canada

Publisher's Cataloging-In-Publication Data
(Prepared by The Donohue Group, Inc.)

Names: Quigley, Dawn, 1970-
Title: Apple in the middle / by Dawn Quigley.
Description: First edition. | Fargo, ND : North Dakota State University Press, [2018] | Series: [Contemporary voices of indigenous peoples] | Interest age level: Young adult.
Identifiers: ISBN 9781946163073
Subjects: LCSH: Indian teenagers--Fiction. | Teenage girls--Fiction. | Stepfamilies--Fiction. | LCGFT: Bildungsromans. | BISAC: YOUNG ADULT FICTION / Family / Blended Families. | YOUNG ADULT FICTION / People & Places / United States / Native American. | YOUNG ADULT FICTION / Coming of Age. | YOUNG ADULT FICTION / Loners & Outcasts.
Classification: LCC PS3617.U5351 A66 2018 | DDC 813/.6 [Fic]--dc23

North Dakota State University Press
Dept. 2360, P.O. Box 6050, Fargo, ND 58108-6050
www.ndsupress.org

To my heart,
to my life,
to my love.

And to my mom and dad: Thank you for showing me the world of reading and stories. You taught me that words can fly me to new places. It's been a wonderful journey so far.

Keep me as the apple of your eye;
hide me in the shadow of your wings.
—Psalm 17

We Are All Connected

Who do I resemble?
I have the eyes of my mother, my beautiful mother, who drinks in the quiet call of the Creator.
My ears are from my grandfather whose heart listens to Mother Nature.
My nose is from my father who covers the scent of human pain.
My mouth is from all my ancestors whose voices still echo.
My heart echoes the beat of the drum.
Within us we carry all our relatives.
We are all connected.

ap·ple (*ap-ul*) noun

1. The usually round, red or yellow, edible fruit of a small tree, *Malussylvestris*, of the rose family.
2. The tree, cultivated in most temperate regions.
3. The fruit of any of certain other species of tree of the same genus.
4. Apple of one's eye: something precious; much loved
5. Slang: *Derogatory term of a* Native American person who . . .

Contents

Prologue

THERE'S A LITTLE GARDEN just outside the back door. I've seen it through the window and I figure it's a safe enough distance from . . . from it. The cemetery. Bouncing down the stairs I take in the deep scent of the Turtle Mountains. The garden is laid out in the shape of a medicine wheel: a circle divided with a cross in the middle. Each quartered section has a plant native to the Turtle Mountain Reservation: sage, clover, and wild roses. But I'm not sure what this fourth plant is. It's in the back part of the garden and towers above everything else. Red berries dot the tall plant—almost like a tree. If it smells as vibrant as it looks my nose will be in for a treat. This little country garden is where I spend time after church when everyone else is up the hill in the cemetery. I won't go up there . . . because, well, *she's* up there.

I get closer to the mystery plant and take a look and sniff. And sniff. And sniff again. I'm going to town trying for the life of me to figure out what this last unknown half tree half bush species is.

"Chokecherry."

"What?" I gasp spinning around.

"Chokecherry. That's what tree yer smellin'. Tree don't smell that good."

I know that voice and it's the last one I want to hear now, "You! . . . but . . ." I stammer, looking frantically around for help.

His black hair looks almost blue with the sun bouncing off it. Over a black t-shirt and camouflaged pants, he's wearing a blaze orange vest. They're together. And they have a gun. Somehow, I think they're big NRA supporters.

He signals to the other, "Back in the truck—I need my scope. This one ain't good for nothin'." And with that the other one starts off back down the road.

Nodding, the one left leans in closer to me, "I was going grouse huntin', but this seems more interestin' here."

His sneer sends a chill up my spine and a warning call down my soul.

Family! Hear me!

My eyes frantically look left and right; where did Grandma say they were? Up the path . . . through the woods . . . to Grandmother's house we go?

No! No! No! Apple, for once in your life think! What was the way Grandma said to find them? What path was I supposed to follow to the cemetery?

"You're not scared, are ya?" He seems to be slowly moving toward me.

"I . . . you . . . what are you doing here?"

"I tol' you, girl. We was huntin'. But I'm the only one here now. Shame." Bending down within inches of my face he continues, "And what are you doing here, Apple?" He says my name like it was tart in his mouth.

"I, well, I . . . we went to church and we decided to . . ."

Looking around, then back at me he slowly realizes, "Oh, I see. You're all alone, my girl. *My girl*."

"Listen," I say as I steadily back up toward the church's clapboard siding trying to put as much distance between us, "I don't know what you have against me . . . and my mom and my family's money for that matter, but —"

"WHAT DO YOU KNOW ABOUT ANYTHING!" His rage is palpable. His pupils constrict as hard as his heart. "You don't know a thing 'bout me. You don't know nothin' 'bout what your ma did to us!" His arms, flailing, emphasize his frenzy.

"Well, seeee, I'm here in the T-Turtle Mountains t-trying to make sense of everything . . . especially my mom —"

He rips the garden plot to shreds with arms thrashing back and forth. Arms tearing at the garden, first grasping a plant, and then he twists the flowers between his massive hands within inches of my face. As the blossoms crush so does my sense of hope.

Trying to calm him I stammer, "This isn't supposed to be like this, you —"

"YOU ain't got NO idea about how things were *supposed* to be."

Backing up against the church's back wall, I dig my feet in as if I thought I might climb up and away. My eyes search for safety.

His gaze sweeps behind him, looking for witnesses. So, this is what a caged animal feels like. This is what prey feels like.

"Well, girl, Apple is a fitting name for the likes of you," he spits. "You're one of them Indians — you're not like the rest of us! Apple — your ma would never have wanted that, Apple."

And then it happens. Again. My visions. Oh, not now! But when they come, there's no stopping them. In my mind, I can barely make out a misty image of this man. From the pit of my soul arise words that rush past my panic and out. Out to confront him.

"When's the last time you all were at the Copa? The Copacabana?" I level off, having no idea what it means.

But apparently, he does. It causes him to stumble back while blinking nonstop. It's just enough of a distraction for me to conjure my escape.

I jab him in the elbow and try to fly around him, leaping into space.

That's the last thing I remember. No, last thing I remember is a sound. I tumble into darkness and a total blackness claims my five senses, except one: my sense of sound. I hear a sound. Then I hear it again.

BANG!

BANG!

And there I am hovering in the middle again, but this time it's between the living and dead.

Chapter 1

SCHOOL. NOT MY FAVORITE thing. Especially the first week back after a glorious summer off. I always dread the first assignment the teachers always have us write: *What I Did Over Summer Vacation*. Seriously. Teachers, this, to us students, is the kiss of death. When you assign that paper, and you always do, we have to hide that fact that most of us did nothing. That most kids can't afford to go anywhere. And even if I won the Nobel Prize for world peace (hey, it could happen), why am I going to spill my personal life to a teacher I don't even know?

I can't help but compare my life to a giant game of keep-away . . . with me always being in the middle running back and forth between two things, never quite catching anything. I call it the Ping-Pong effect because you're the ball, and nobody ever wants you in their space. Have you ever felt like that? Never really belonging anywhere, but trying your darndest to run between two lives only to find you're always stuck in the middle?

Well that's the *Reader's Digest* summary of my life: Apple in the Middle. Did I tell you that *I'm* Apple? Yes, my name is the same as a fruit. How I got that name is coming later. I promise. I'll get to the "how I spent my summer vacation" story later *AND* the story behind my name. I promise I will. I'm nothing, if not honest.

First, you should know that I tend to have some *minor* odd habits. For one, and some might call it a phobia, but I call it common sense that I will *not* step foot into a cemetery. There's just something about stepping and hovering above decomposing bodies. Nope. Won't do it. What if a boney skeleton hand reaches up and pulls me under? It's really all about staying on this side of the turf. Cemeteries smell kind of funky, too. Eau de decay. Plus, I'm afraid that a dearly departed may want to exact a little revenge.

Another peculiar habit of mine is that I love asking people odd questions. It's not that I need to or want to ask the questions, but it's a tic. It's almost like I get a thought in my head and it can't stay in there quietly. The questions just pop into my head and when they do, I just blurt them out. It may sound weird, but sometimes when I talk to people, I get this hazy vision of them in my head. Usually it's some image of them doing things. I don't have any reference about them and can't figure out why I get these visions. And they usually get me in trouble. Of course.

Once I was talking to my high school English teacher, Ms. Katerwall, and an image of her popped in my head. Ms. Katerwall is one of those teachers who are book snobs. Book snobs can list every title that they've read. They know every author from A to Z. They also love to make you feel inferior if they see you reading your horoscope in the newspaper. Hey, I need to read the horoscopes (I'm an Aquarius, by the way) to see if I'll "meet my dream man" today, or if I should "wait before making big decisions."

As I'm asking her about an English assignment I start to get a vision, or mental image, of her in a bathtub (don't worry, she has bubbles up to her bulbous nose), and she's reading a book and laughing to herself. So, in the middle of English class while all the normal kids are working on a writing assignment (BTW, I really hate to write) I blurt out and ask her, "Do you always read comic books in the bathtub, Ms. Katerwall?" Let's just say that didn't go over well. A book snob would never be caught dead reading Calvin and Hobbes. I told you. I have odd habits.

But I can't help myself. It's like I have no filter on my mouth. Whenever these pictures, or images, pop in my head, some stupid comment pops out. It's like having a really bad case of diarrhea of the mouth. I wonder if there's a Pepto Mismol for loose junk escaping my mouth. This quirk of mine does nothing to fill my social calendar.

Just for interest, sometimes when I talk to people an English accent stammers out, or maybe an Australian "shrimp on the barbie" may come out of nowhere. I wish I could say that my friends think I'm the weird, but lovable, goof. I can't say that . . . because I have no friends. That's right (sob, sniff, tear drop). Maybe people are afraid of my exuberance, odd questions, and spotty Russian accent, so they stare at me whenever I pass them by. I'm pretty sure I see sympathy looks too. I do this because it's better to be singled out as the weird foreign kid than to be known for being the weird freaky local kid.

I don't have to worry about losing any friends by acting odd because I . . . well . . . always feel out of place; never have really had friends; and am even shunned by my little brother. I use my talents for speaking with accents and take on the pretend role of foreign exchange student. My high school is so big that it's impossible to know everyone in your grade. This solves my problems and gives a reason for my lackluster personal life.

If I'm in fourth-hour lunch making my way to the lunch line, I may "accidentally" bump into people, preferably juniors or seniors who don't know of my existence and say, "Oopps, sooorry, I 'ad better check my shrimp in back at the boats, mate!" The bewildered looks they shoot back at me read: "Hello, too weird, wait, I detect an accent . . . maybe there's a reason for her bizarreness . . ."

With my brown hair (mousy black) and brown (mud) eyes I can slide into numerous identities. Maybe during the Monday meatloaf lunch hour I'll be a whispery waif from Ukraine, or on Tuesday with tacos (Toxic Smell lunch day), I'll be a Latina from an obscure Spanish-speaking country. I feel *sort* of bad because one poor sap I tried my Spanish accent on actually believed that I was from a country called "El Burrit-o." And these are the kids that will lead our country into the future? Yikes. But I figure it's better to be a weird foreigner than a pathetic loser.

Looking on the bright side, when you're socially invisible people don't realize you're watching them. It's sort of one of my favorite pastimes: people watching, especially when they have no idea you exist.

Sometimes it's good to be unseen, which is why I like to people watch. I can do this anytime, but it's especially fun when I'm in Math class with Mr. Markman. By the way, Mr. Markman is obsessed with the scent of whiteboard markers (not sure if I want to know anything more about that), so his back is always toward the class. You may not be able to *see* him, but you can *hear* him taking deep halting breaths as he scribbles notes on the whiteboard. Last month I got in trouble because I accidently called him *Mr. Marker-man* to his face, but that's another story.

So during his class I have a back row, corner desk, which is a prime spot for viewing the high schoolers. I get a glimpse of the different groups of kids and get to peek into their lives. You know all groups, they're in every school since time immortal: the jocks (or as I call them, "the grunts" because that seems to be the only response anyone gets to questions they ask them), the ultra-pretty girls (also known as "two-fers" because they make every one-syllable word into two. For example, if I tell them their shoes are "so last year," instead of saying, "what?," two-fers say, "Whu-ut?"), the geeks (or as I call them, "the geeks"), and the motorheads (who know nothing about nineteenth-century British poetry, but can dismantle and reassemble a 1956 GT faster than you could say blue collar career).

As I observe the natives I fill out a journal. I figure if I can't be a *part* of high school society, then I'll document my observations for future generations. My journal is divided into chapters.

Chapter one: How many days in a row can our football team not bring anything to class? No notebook, no pencils, no textbook. So far they're up to 157. It technically should be 158 days in a row, but I had to give credit for last Tuesday when Paul Dougan and Brian Whirth came into class chewing a pencil eraser. I'm nothing if not fair. I also keep a running tally of how many times Steve Jernow turns and smirks at me when I say something in class. Every. Single. Time. And, of course, Al Tuffs doesn't help the team's count as he digs in the garbage for notebook paper. Usually I give him credit for foraging, but he sometimes catches me watching him. I'm not sure if he's the president of the "Who Thinks Apple is Weird?" fan club, but he's at least the secretary (it's a common fact that they give that job to the biggest dolt).

I guess you could call some of these guys handsome, if you're into that sort of thing. Of course I couldn't care less about them; I just wish they wouldn't always laugh. Foreign exchange students have feelings, too.

Back to my journal . . .

Chapter two: Does Marcia Glasglow (the queen of all two-fers) wear the same outfit twice? This chapter really is more of an Excel graphing sheet which documents Marcia's outfits. One thing I should be really good at is recognizing designer clothes. I may have no social life, but we're loaded (thanks to my dad being a surgeon) so I have a pretty killer wardrobe. Except, I sort of mix up designer chic with Walmart geek, but it seems to work for me. It may even be better than Marcia's outfits, but who's keeping track? Technically, I guess *I* am.

Chapter three. This is my favorite chapter so far: Top Ten Secret Moves to see if the teacher is watching you. If you must know, the top moves are: the "yawn-stretch-turn-your-head" move, the "wipe your chin on your shoulder and look" move, and then my personal favorite, the "glance at the clock and quickly look at teacher" move.

So far, after writing about these observations over the course of my high school career I've learned about watching people, studying people, and analyzing their behavior. But I still can't figure out the one thing I really want. Where do I fit? Where do I belong?

Last week at lunch I found an empty table next to the founding members of the two-fers, Marcia Glasglow. She saw me trying to save my soupy applesauce from sliding next to my chicken nuggets. I *might* have freaked out a little bit (OK, I hyperventilated). I hate when food touches. What's wrong with food segregation? Don't want my peas touching my pasta, or my meatloaf mingling with my melon. Marcia watched me from the next table and giggled. It started to roll from that into an all-out eye-crying, hold-her-chest laughing hysteric.

"Oh my *go-osh*, Apple," she yelled so everyone could hear. "Wha-at do you think you're doing? Keeping your applesauce from touching you — a *real* Apple? That's like, that's like cannibalism!"

Yeah, good one Marcia. But of course, this is what sticks in people's minds whenever they see me eat lunch now at school, which is why I sometimes eat in the closet next to the teacher's lounge. Remind me to tell you some of the things I hear floating through the vents while they're eating. Whoa, some serious issues. And *they're* teaching *us*?

Marcia, queen of mean, is the one person I try to avoid at school. I want to be invisible around her. Most times I can hide, but in the middle of the lunchroom on that horrible day last week, up bubbled one of my quirky questions. It's like the words simmer in my stomach, and then bypass my mind erupting over my tongue. *Please, please. Not now. Not the questions with* her.

"Eye ate teen?" I asked as applesauce dripped down my mouth.

"Ex-cuuuse me?" she shrieked. Her eyes were wild as they scanned the room to see who was watching.

"Be-fore?" Crud — it's happening again. Who knows what I even mean? Do I have Tourette's Syndrome?

"Apple, you are one *weird* fruit." And with that Marcia shook her head and dismissed my question . . . and my existence. My humiliation is complete. But not quite. I saw someone sitting next to her who was chuckling at me. Most kids turned their attention back to the barf-tastic burrito lunch. Everyone except the football team. Must I always have witnesses for every humiliation?

Chapter 2

THE SCHOOL BUS. I'M fifteen and friendless. Need I say more? The ride home this afternoon was average: kids throwing backpacks on empty seats yelling, "Taken!" signaling me to keep moving; juice "accidently" spills on me as I pass; and yet I get an "hola!" from someone who feels sorry for the foreign exchange girl. Gracias.

Looking out the bus window, I think about school. I live forty minutes from my school. Not a big thing, you may think, but again, it sets me up for bouncing in the middle between two more things: home and school.

Back when I was in grade school the kids on my block would talk about the big neighborhood whiffle ball game the night before. But I could never play with those kids who lived next to me because there wasn't time with all of the driving back and forth we did between school and home.

I never was able to play with my classmates from school either, because we lived forty miles away in a "gated community." For some reason, my dad didn't want me to attend the private prep school in our small town. He said it was too elitist and snobby. So, he thought bussing me off to the public school the next town over would be better. Yeah, thanks, Dad. Riding a bus for forty-five minutes with hot sweaty kids is my dream. I didn't go to the prep school, so the neighborhood kids thought I was being a dork and wouldn't give me the time of day. And the kids at school assumed I was a rich snob because of where I lived, so they didn't invite me over.

Me in the middle of two worlds. Again.

Here's another shocker: I don't look *anything* like the other girls at school. They are blond, blue-eyed, and have perfect cream-colored complexions. There's not much diversity at my school, but there's a small Hispanic population in town, so a few "students of color" (that's what my principal calls them) attend school with me. And then there's me, too dark to fit in with the white girls and too English speaking to fit in with the Latina girls. See? Even my *outside* is in the middle.

Let me explain a little bit about being in the middle. Now I'm not talking about being the middle child. Yeah, yeah, yeah, I get it: The middle child is usually the peacemaker who is the middle man between the eldest over-achieving child and the youngest brat. The middle child shields the youngest child from wedgie and noogie attacks. No. I'm not *that* type of middle. Let me explain why I'm Apple-in-the-middle.

I've always felt like I'm living and bouncing between two worlds: the white and the Native American, with nowhere to comfortably land. Being different, I ricochet back and forth everywhere else, too, from family life, friendships, school, and my appearance.

I remember the first time I realized I was different. *Really* different. It was springtime and I was nine years old playing during recess. At that time in my life I loved being outside. I used to spend so much time outside that my naturally tanned skin would turn black as night in the warmer months. Outdoors was the one place I might possibly find someone to play with. When you're that age, you don't even care if you know someone's name, you just all play together. Or so I thought.

I was at the top of the slide on our school playground waiting for the kid ahead of me to go down when I could hear someone yelling. At first, I couldn't make out what the kid was saying. It took me a few seconds to figure out he was yelling at *me*.

But then I caught it.

A boy—and I have to say he was really ugly with an upturned nose and a unibrow—turned to his friends behind him and thrust his chin up to me, as if drawing their attention upward. "Hey, *prairie nigger*," ugly boy yelled, "get off the slide!"

Did he just call me *that*? I was so stunned that I did the only thing I knew how to do. I hocked a loogie on him. A big one.

That phrase. I've heard grown-ups use the "N" word. But what he called me—*prairie nigger*—is only spewed at Native Americans. That day the boy took away something from me. He took away my love of the outdoors. He took away the one place I felt I belonged. He took away the hidden half that my mother gave me, the Indian side, and replaced it with shame. Which is why, of course, I spit a juicy loogie on him.

I ran home that afternoon, my nine-year-old face wet with tears of shame. I knew my dad, the doctor, was home because he had Mondays off. As early as I could remember my dad kept to himself a lot. In the house. With his buddy, Jim. Jim Beam. I could smell that liquor on my dad from a mile away. So, if I had a problem, I needed to fix it.

He was surprised to see me, and looked up from his newspaper, and his drink.

"Apple, what are you doing home so soon?"

And I slowly spilled my playground tale. At hearing the phrase "prairie nigger," my dad's eye contact broke, and he looked past my shoulders, gazing at some unseen vista. And he stayed there, like he always did when the subject of my mother came up—or anything Indian. He eventually focused back on me and tried to comfort me the only way he knew how.

"See, what that boy really needs to understand is that humans truly share 99.998 percent of the same genotypes and chromosomes. It's that last 0.002 percent which makes us only seem different and results in varying skin tones, eye color, and the shape and texture of hair."

I just looked at him while he tried to explain away my hurt. Except what *he* didn't understand, and never did, is that there isn't a rational way to explain away an injured ego or a sad soul.

And ever since that day, I've always worn a hat outside and have been religious about applying sunscreen so my skin wouldn't get any darker. Being different is something I just hated. I've never told anyone else what happened to me that day. You're the first. I guess I felt that if I didn't say this aloud, then it never really happened.

After ugly unibrow boy lobbed the words that pierced my heart, thus began the starting point of my fascination with inventing ways to keep me out of the direct sunlight. I figured if I didn't fit in, then at least my skin would look like every other pasty pale-skinned Minnesotan. I wanted my legs to look lefse-white. Every other mother in America is chasing their kids around with SPF nine-hundred trying to rub layers of sunscreen on the arms, face, and legs of their precious ones. I decided that I wouldn't let the sun touch my skin. No sun. No tan. No more names. No more standing out. Everyone within miles of me had white, I'm talking *lily* white skin, so pale you can see their *soul* white, so in my mind if I could just look like them, I could be like them. If I could *be* like them, then they'd have to invite me to join in all their reindeer games.

I grew up having to figure out how to take care of myself, because, until his new wife, Judy, came along, my dad was still trying to figure how to forgive me for my mom's death.

She had to leave this life because I had to come. You think *that's* a huge emotional obstacle to overcome? I'll let you in on one juicier tidbit about me: I killed my mother. But more on that later.

And it's probably why that day I buried the fact that I'm half Indian, from my mom, and repressed it whether consciously or not. And that was also the same day that my odd question habit emerged.

* * *

My school district tries to be multicultural, which, considering everyone except me and a few others are white, is always interesting. I am the Oreo crumb floating in a glass of milk.

Back in first grade we put on a play about "The First Thanksgiving." Now this was before what I refer to as the "third-grade playground issue," and so any chance I had to learn more about Native Americans I jumped at it. It's sad to think that in order to learn about who I was, I had to get it from any place outside of my home. My dad, whenever I asked about my Indian side, always gazed past me and got lost somewhere in his thoughts, in his sadness.

So, all of us first-graders got to choose which character we wanted to play. (Do teachers still actually *do* the stereotypical November "Indian" unit? Probably. Do they know we Natives are alive all year long? Not just November?) Most boys wanted to be Miles Standish and the girls wanted to be some noble Pilgrim wife (like I'd want to re-enact washing my husband's drawers without a Maytag? Not).

Me? I wanted to be Squanto: friendly Indian guide. Of course, *now* I know that Squanto was really born Tisquantum from the Patuxet tribe, and he was actually *kidnapped*, sold into slavery in Europe, and when returned all of his family and entire tribe was wiped out by disease. Really! But still, I was only in first grade, and I knew he was the only part for me! Seriously teachers, read some history. At first my teacher told me that girls *cannot* play boy parts. Of course, I reminded her that Shakespeare allowed boys to play girl parts (my dad may have his issues, but ever the scholar, he taught me a few things that came in handy), and so who is she to go against that?

Yeah, that teacher really loved a six-year-old putting her in her place. And that's how I got to play the Indian hero, Squanto, in our play. Of course, everyone else picked playing a Pilgrim. Plymouth Plantation score: fifty-two Pilgrims and one Indian. No wonder the Native people had no chance for survival.

The day of the big production came and I was ready. I made a vest out of a paper bag—something my art teacher helped me make—braided my hair, and donned a crow feather that I found on the way to school in my hair. To me, I looked Indian, but the expression on my dad's face when I peered out from the stage told me otherwise. It was as if he was embarrassed of my appearance. And afterwards, walking out to the car, he took my paper vest and feather and threw them in the trash. He did it so gently, but never explained why. Whenever I would attempt to try to be Indian it brought up a sadness in him, but I, being a child, interpreted it as shame.

After my first-grade year I quit trying to be Indian, whatever that was. I'd already lost my mom, and I didn't want to drive away my dad. He's all I had left, so I pushed away searching for exterior ways to be Native American. And it seemed to work, until that day on the playground in third grade when the boy called me "prairie nigger."

School—a little bit of my own personal hell. In more ways than one.

Chapter 3

SO AT THE DINNER table on the last day of school my tenth-grade year, my dad and stepmom, Judy, are acting very weird, more so than usual. Like, why did they set out the good china? Why were the lights dimmed? Why did they make my younger stepbrother, Baer, put on pants before he came to the table? What I didn't know was that this was a "send off" dinner. It was me they were sending off for the summer—the *whole* summer—only I didn't know it.

"Apple," my dad starts, "what are your plans for the summer?"

"Yesss, dear, now I think it would be good if you visited—" Judy begins to say.

"Well, Ed," I cut in, but as soon as I see he-whose-face-would-turn cement, I change my tune. "Dad, I'm thinking of . . . umm . . . well, see . . . my plans are in motion . . ."

What can I say? I have *no* idea what my summer plans are. I *never* have summer plans that don't include: running (away from the pesky brother Baer), swimming (in a boat-load of spending money that I call my dad's "guilt offering" after his years with Jim Beam), and just plain relaxing (after a school year trying desperately to fit in, but never quite making it).

I look back and forth between my dad and Judy. There's something going on. Usually Judy jumps when I look around the table, thinking I need something.

My dad continues, "Apple, Judy and I were thinking."

I look up from my mountain of peas (which are blissfully parted away from my chicken. I really don't like my food to touch. Ever.). "You were thinking? That's good, Dad."

"Well, yes. You know every summer I need to go back to the University of Minnesota Medical School for its annual conference."

"Yeah, Dad. Baer and I will promise not to fight this time over who gets to keep the gift bags if they have models of cancer-ridden organs."

Baer spits his food out, adding, "But, Dad, that tar-covered lung last year was *awesome*!"

Judy chimes in, "Now, kidssssss, your father is trying to talk." My stepmom has a sibilant s, so when she speaks it sounded like a tea pot whistling Dixie. If she gets really wound up, her "s-es" would attract all the neighborhood birds. Seriously. Once a blue jay plowed into our living room window trying to fly to her sibilant s. For some reason, I was the only one who found that funny. She caused a bird to commit suicide, that's funny, right?

"So," Dad continues while looking at Baer and me, "this year Judy and I were thinking that you could spend time with your grandparents." Since he's looking at Baer, too, I'm assuming he means Judy's parents.

Lame. Judy's parents, Mae and Jed Silver, are the only grandparents I really know, since my dad's passed away before I knew them. Don't get me wrong, I like Judy's folks and everything, even if technically they're my stepgrandparents, or something like that. But they're missionaries . . . out on a mission. Their mission seems to be a bit off, though. Last year they sent swim floaties and goggles to the starving children of Africa. Yes, that Africa, where there is little water to swim in.

"Great," I choke out. "Grandma and Grandpa Silver are . . . ummm . . . so wholesome."

Dad stammers, "Well now, Apple, Baer will go there, but we were thinking . . ."

"Yes, dear, we were *hoping* . . ." Judy whispers almost inaudibly.

"That you should want to go visit your grandparents . . . in North Dakota."

I just sat and stared at my dad. What did he just say?

"I'm sorry, what? *Who* should I visit?"

He pats me on the head with a defeated look in his eyes. "Well, it's just important that you get to know your mother's side, Apple."

Since I didn't belong to any social scene, I only put up a pretend teen protest when the dinner table conversation turns into my dad suggesting I spend some "quality time" (read: they want a reprieve from me) with various relatives. I can't believe it. They're giving me the boot!

Now, don't get me wrong, who doesn't like spending time with Grandma and Pa? Except for the fact that I haven't seen my grandparents since my mom died. Actually, I've never seen them.

Remember I told you that? Ya, my mom, real mom, died when I was born. I wish I could remember her, but whenever I ask questions about her my dad says, "Oh Apple, let's not bring that up, it will upset you."

Oh, that's right. I promised I'd tell you why I am named after a fruit.

Apparently, the story goes like this:

My real mother went into early labor when she was only eight months pregnant with me. She got into a bad car accident, and had to be rushed to the Mayo Clinic in Rochester, Minnesota (where my dad used to work as a surgeon and the town where Mom taught school). It's a famous world-renowned hospital where only the seriously ill patients go.

Because of the trauma of the car crash, my mom started to go into labor quickly. Luckily, I wasn't injured during the crash. But she was. She died exactly eleven minutes after I was born. I came into this world just as she was leaving.

My dad only told me this once because he *never* talks about her. Never. He did, however, let me know the last thing my mom ever said was something like, "*Ma fille, la pomme de mes yeauxs.*" That's supposedly a bad and rough translation in French for: *My girl, the apple of my eye.*

Why was my mom speaking French? See, my mom grew up in a little town in North Dakota called Morinville. It's fourteen miles from the Canadian border and smack dab in the middle of the Turtle Mountain Chippewa Indian Reservation. Yep, she was a real live Native American. She actually spent a lot of time with her grandmother from the time she was two years old. The brief and simple history of this reservation is that its people are descended from Chippewa Indians and French fur traders, so they have a mixed heritage. I guess a lot of people on that reservation used to speak both French and the local dialect of the Chippewa, or the correct term, Ojibwe. Her parents worked all week, so during the day my mom's grandma would babysit.

Mom's grandmother, Elizabeth, spoke *Michif*, language which is a blend of Cree and French, with some Ojibwe words thrown in for good measure. The mixed band of Natives were called *Metis*, the French word for mixed, but the tribe also calls themselves Michif. It's confusing a little, but I sort of like having more than one name to call yourself. On this reservation, the French words aren't pronounced the same. Their French words sound different, same spelling, but a distinct way of saying them. The internet says the Turtle Mountain Michif is the only Native language in America that's a creole, or mixture, of language—sorry, I need to stay on track.

Grandma Elizabeth also spoke French. Which makes sense that my mother spoke French before she even spoke her first English word. Mom could navigate between the Michif language and French, and always knew which was which, my dad says. I remember everything he's ever told me about her. It's not much, but it's all I have.

I've heard that when people are about to die their mind works backwards and the person starts reverting back to their first language. My mother's native tongue was Michif and French. In a nutshell, that's why my mother's last words weren't in English. Back to that story . . .

After Mom gave birth to me, the nurse cleaned me up and laid me on her stomach. Those in the operating room said my mother looked at me and laughed while saying something that sounded like, "*Ma fille, la pomme de mes yeauxs.*" *My girl, the apple of my eye.* (One time last year I asked my French teacher if this sounded like the right phrase. She said she didn't think so, but wasn't sure.)

In the delivery room the nurse who was holding my mom's hand understood enough rudimentary high school French and somehow, after my mom passed away a few minutes later, took it to mean my name was supposed to be *Apple*. Nice.

What really upsets me is having to pretend that my real mom never existed. I want to ask if people remember her the way my images of her are:

"Did the room really get brighter when she walked in?"

"Did she really have magic in her voice that made your heart warm instantly?"

"Did her eyes laugh when she saw me?"

And finally, "Do you blame me for her death?"

A million unanswered questions.

This story, the only one that my dad would tell me, became an obsession. I couldn't get over the fact that my mom was dead. In a box. Rotting away in a grave. Mixing with worms and dirt. Which is why I never, *ever* step foot in a cemetery. The thought of decaying bodies just inches from the surface nauseates me. The last time my dad tried to take me to a funeral I screamed bloody murder when they lowered the casket in the grave. I spun around and did hopscotch moves jumping over tombstones to avoid dead earth. You *could* say I have issues, but I prefer to say it's just part of my charm.

* * *

Passing the lasagna around at the big sendoff dinner, and after giving a meaningful glance at Judy, my dad sighs and tries again. "Apple, it's high time you spend time with your mother's family. Your *real* grandparents. I . . . I want you to get to know them. This summer will be the perfect opportunity. Judy and I will be away in Minneapolis organizing the conference, and Baer will still be going to his grandparents'. Judy and I were hoping to do some traveling after the conference. Sort of like the honeymoon we never had. So . . ." Dad looks at me, "Apple, maybe when you're up there, and feel able to, you can visit your mother's gravesite—"

"No!" I cut him off. He can't go *there*. Not the grave thing. Not *hers*. "You know . . . I just, well, cemeteries, and gravesites, are . . . well . . . I can't do it. I'm really sorry, Dad."

I can't believe what he's saying! For years he wouldn't even acknowledge my mother's name. He couldn't even answer questions about what my mom looked like, sounded like, acted like. And now he wants me to be *happy* to spend time with people I don't even know?

. . . and who probably blame me for the death of their daughter?

. . . and yet, I might finally get some answers?

. . . and could I actually meet people who look like me?

So, I said the only thing I could, after swallowing and hiding my pain at the thought of my mother in a grave: "When do we leave," and "Do they have cable?"

Chapter 4

I'M GOING TO SEE my grandparents. *I* am going to see my grandparents. After all these years, all these questions ago, I'll finally get some answers. Now the BIG question: what to pack?

As I walk to my bedroom to pack I realize that I'm going to miss it this summer. Dad picked this house out right after my mom died. He and Judy married only a year and a half later. It was really Judy who helped my dad quit drinking over time. Bye-bye. Jim Beam. Baer, who technically is my stepbrother, came with Judy. So, we've been here a while—booze-free—but little brother seems to give me a hangover each and every day.

Our house is a seven-bedroom, five-bath house with seven thousand square feet, a behemoth of the neighborhood. We live on Lake Minnetonka, where all the old-Minnesota-money families park their palatial abodes. Lake Minnetonka is the fourth largest lake in the state, but you can't even buy a house on its shores for under a cool million. Minnetonka is only about twelve miles from the city of Minneapolis, but it's really worlds away economically. You'd think with all this money my dad rakes in, I could make friends with at least someone around here who might want to hang out with the daughter of the famous (or infamous . . . I can't ever remember the difference) doctor.

Back in my room I'm sitting on my bed amid an ocean of clothes. What does one wear when first meeting an Indian? I ask Judy what I should wear when she ambles in with more laundry; she may be annoying, but she has a good fashion eye.

"So Judes, have you ever met an Indian before?" I ask.

"Well, I did read Gandhi's biography lasssst winter," she replies while piling up more clothes into my suitcase, her sibilant s calling out to the birds.

"No, Judy, the other kind. The *American* kind." How did Judy ever make it through nursing school? Good thing she quit working after marrying my dad or she could have caused an international incident.

"Well," she continues, "let'sss sssee. How many American Indians do I know?" Judy looked up at the ceiling while mentally counting on her fingers. "I guess there's . . . just you, Apple."

Wow. I just about had the wind knocked out of me. I guess technically I am Indian, but I just never think about it anymore. It's like one half of me is hidden, the Indian part and I know nothing about it.

It's funny to think about me being Native American, American Indian . . . which means I will definitely pack my "rodeo girl" look clothes. Throw some jeans on me and I'm ready to go. Giddy up.

* * *

We pack up the Land Rover and head out on I-94 up past Fargo, then drive due north to Morinville, North Dakota. Morinville, home of "maybe I'll get some answers" North Dakota.

The farther out I get from Minneapolis area, the more anxious I get. Isn't seeing cows and hay fields supposed to be calming and relaxing? What's up with that? And what's up with this *smell*? Oh, cancel that; it's just Baer next to me in the car. How can boys smell so much? Dad and Judy are dropping him off last in Minot, North Dakota, after me. Apparently, North Dakota is eating young like there's no tomorrow.

This whole time since we've left home my dad and Judy keep looking back at me, checking to see if I'm having nervous breakdown. Funny, but I don't feel anything yet. So I just smile at them and crank my music even louder.

Leaning my head on the window, I wonder what should I be feeling? Should I be nervous? I'm just meeting the parents of my mother. My mother who died because of me. What if I have made a colossal mistake? Jeeves, turn this heap around! I know what I'm feeling, and it isn't good.

All of a sudden, I feel my body full of nerves. I think I've made a huge mistake, and apparently so do the hot and spicy cheese puffs I ate for lunch because they have erupted past my mouth and into Baer's lap. He takes one look at the puddle of puke and starts his own Mount Vesuvius. Right into the back of Judy's head.

Houston, we have a problem.

* * *

After we pull over, clean up, and fumigate the Land Rover we're back on our merry way. Except I'm not feeling too merry about this. But I really need to get out of this car and away from the faint whiff of cheese puff.

I've got my iPod cranked again when I look out the window as we pass a massive sign reading,

WELCOME TO THE TURTLE MOUNTAIN CHIPPEWA INDIAN RESERVATION

Underneath it someone spray-painted in fluorescent green, "Whites need not apply." Yikes.

Don't ask me why, but suddenly I have the urge to look up at the sky. For some reason, I sort of thought I'd see an eagle or two soaring above. And maybe hear some flute music. Isn't that what always happens on TV when Indians show up? But no such luck.

Looking out the window I notice this isn't the lush landscape I pictured when I thought of "Indian Reservation." It surprises me because I thought I would be seeing majestic pines and towering oaks mingling with poplars and birch trees. Instead, this is just the opposite. There is little to no prairie grass or shady groves of trees. I see scrub brush and prickly-looking plants littering the land next to the small highway as we make our way farther into reservation territory. I'm pretty sure I see one of those tumbleweeds cartwheel across the road, too. The land starts to gently slope into slight hills as we make our way to Morinville, North Dakota, just five miles into the border of the Turtle Mountain Reservation.

We finally pull into the little town. Apparently, it's the home of "1967, 1968, 1969, and 1970 State Basketball Champions" as the sign states in peeling paint. I'm a bit worried. Has nothing good happened here since 1970?

We're looking for the address: 2905 Rose Place. Dad remembers coming here a few times after he and my mom got married and finds the address in no time. They were only married four years before she . . . before she . . . you know. I came along then, too.

Turning off the main highway the car continues to bring me closer to my past, but my stomach has other ideas. Baer hears my gut churn and looks at me with a glare that could kill.

"D-A-D! Open the windows, quick! Apple's gonna blow again!"

"Oh, chill," I calmly reply, "I'm just hungry (*such a lie*)." My stomach is churning with a mix of nausea and nerves, with little bits of licorice floating around.

Dad bellows, "Both of you! Just . . . just . . . oh. Here's the road right here."

The long narrow gravel road we turn at is flanked on either side by a group of pine trees. The mailbox at the end of the driveway is a rusted out tiny tractor balancing on top of a rotted tree stump. Surrounding it are hundreds of miniature rosy flowers somehow turning the rotting corpse of a mailbox into a scene worthy of a postcard. Back woods sort of beauty, I guess.

"Apple, it's just around the bend!" Dad says.

I close my eyes, not wanting my image spoiled by the truth. *Please, please, Mom. Show yourself to me.*

We must have arrived because the car stops. With my eyes still shut I hear Judy and Baer inhale quickly.

"It's . . . colorful," she says.

"It's . . . cozy," Baer adds.

"It's a . . . PINK . . . TRAILER," I spit out after I open my eyes.

My mind never imagined this. I thought maybe it would be a log cabin nestled between tall pines. Or perhaps an old farm house standing in what was once the family acreage. But this? This *can't* be where my mom grew up. Dare I say it, but was she . . . trailer trash? Mom, who are you?

But I don't have a second to ruminate on this because right then I notice a gaggle of people on a deck off of the trailer (did I mention that it was pink, Flamingo pink, Pepto Bismol pink?). But instead of running out to meet us and yelling over each other as they greeted their long-lost granddaughter . . . they just sit there. And rock in their chairs. And stare at us. Rock and stare.

My dad sighs a deep breath of courage, unbuckles, and tumbles back in time as he opens the door to his past. In slow motion, we all followed suit.

We get out. And stare. They just sit. And stare. If only I could have harnessed all this carbon dioxide as everyone exhales. It could solve the oil crisis with plenty left over.

"Your front tires are low," one of the Indian people on the deck finally says after what seems like ages.

This is the first thing I hear from my long-lost clan? That the car is riding low? Not, "Oh, Apple. You're here! Now our life is complete."

Whoever said American Indians were a wise, unassuming, or kind people apparently have never met these Indians. But I'm getting all of my information from TV — never a good thing.

Chapter 5

THE REASON I MOVE away from the Land Rover is not that I am drawn to my Indian folk, my people, my tribe (dare I say my "peeps"?), but that Baer is starting to dry heave. It's really more of a life survival skill that I get as far from him as possible. My stomach will not taste another cheese-flavored snack as long as I live. OK, maybe I'll just take a break for a while. At least until Dad can get the car detailed again.

As I step farther from the car the first thing that assaults my senses is that smell. A sweet smell. Well, it's just a reprieve to get out of our stench-a-saurus. But as I step out I inhale (solely on the basis of instinct) and smell something so foreign, so striking that I'm speechless. And this is saying a lot. Not physically being able to utter anything is not what I'm used to. I just stand, with the car behind me, and sniff. And sniff. And sniff again.

Being from the city, I'm familiar with the scent of garbage in the morning, the perfume of exhaust fumes drifting in from the freeway, and my personal favorite aroma—melting tar from parking lots. That's what my nose is at ease with.

But here, I step outside and inhale the fresh smell of fields never touched by development, the delicateness of pollen never polluted by fertilizer. Never in my life have I smelled something so amazing, but then I look back to the pink trailer, and my senses reel me back to reality.

My family is slowly shutting the car doors as we make our way up the crumbling sidewalk to the deck. As far as I can see, no one is getting up yet. This is awkward. I'm starting to feel really self-conscious. And nervous. Doesn't anyone want me? Here I am again in the middle. In the middle of two families—one from the past and one from the present. I look back at my dad as he shrugs and gives me a sheepish grin. One that says, "sorry."

This is quite possibly the most embarrassing situation I've ever been in. And when I get anxious my mind takes over. It must be some ancient tribal survival protection mode. I should politely introduce myself and my family. But who are we kidding? I have a track record for oddness.

I walk to the bottom of the steps, clear my throat and say, "Allo! Cry-kie! Y'all have a right nice double-wide. Does she come with a barbie for grillin' the shrimp?"

Yes, I revert to my foreign exchange student like I do every time I stress out. What else could I do? It's either hold my ground here (as a Sheila from Down Under) or go back in the vomit mobile.

At that moment, there was a racket in the back row of the Indian audience. I can hear a chair scraping as we all look in that direction. Either the cheese puffs are doing a number on my vision, or I see a mountain walking toward me. Something so large, so mammoth, that it's blocking out the sun. I'm still squinting trying to make out what massive form is pounding out step-by-step toward me.

OK, so it's not a mountain. But it is the largest person I've ever seen. He looks to be about twenty-five years old and pushing the scale at four hundred pounds. With every thundering step he takes, a waterfall of blue-black hair swings behind him.

I watch him. My family watches him. His family watches him.

From behind me I can hear Baer whisper the phrase from his favorite professional wrestling show, "Let's get ready to rumble!"

At the end of the deck, right in front of me, the-man-who-would-be-mountain finally stops punishing the wooden steps underneath him and plants his feet. Crossing his arms (the size of cannons, I might add), he stares at me. He glares at me from head to toe.

As I glance back at my dad, I can see him starting to give me a look of defeat. Dad starts to turn around and head back to the car. But he stops dead in his tracks when the mountain opens his mouth.

Everyone, both red and white, gives the mountain our full attention.

The mountain turns back to his clan, sweeps a glare to my family, then sets his eyes on me, winks, and says, "G'day, mate."

With that this lumbering giant starts a grin so wide it rips apart the chasm of both families. The Indian crowd opens a torrent of laughter and yells, "Junior, come back up here!" just as my family sighs relief.

As the laughter dies down and we all catch our breath, I take a closer look at the group sitting on the deck. Some have resumed talking quietly amongst themselves, which makes me think they are "minor" relatives that are here to see me, but maybe not to welcome me. The mountain-sized man is chatting back on the porch.

Then I see another couple. They haven't taken their eyes off me and look at me with such a gentle gaze that I know exactly who they are. I know love when I see it. And I'll take all I can get.

These two people are getting up from their chairs. They vaguely resemble an old photo my dad gave me years ago of my mom's parents. The first one getting up is an older woman, maybe in her sixties, is wearing an apron, is short and stocky, and is slightly overweight with a mass of salt and pepper waves shaped closely to her head. Her skin is the color of cinnamon (not like Cinnabons, that's much too dark), with a soft ripple of wrinkles sprinkled about her face. She has a faint curl of a grin fighting to stay quiet.

The other person getting up is an older man, maybe in his sixties, too, with a thick mass of jet-black hair. Standing over six feet tall with a trim build, he sets his pipe back on the table next to him as he stands. He turns and says something to the woman wearing the apron, and everyone on the deck laughs. For a second, I'm sure that they're laughing on my account. But I see him slowly look at me, and his face softens to a calming smile settling the storm. My storm.

"Apple," he says, "come give your mooshum, your *grandfather*, a hug."

The woman in the apron, who I assume is my grandmother, says, "Come here, my girl."

My dad walks back to me and murmurs softly in my ear, "Apple, I sense you'll fit in just fine. Do you think you will be OK?"

I smile, look up at him and whisper back with a little crack in my voice, "Dad, they had me at G'day."

* * *

My dad needs to do something to fill the awkward silence, so he starts unpacking the car. I may have over packed a bit. A good packer plans for all occasions: weddings, funerals, cotillions, sailboat regattas, and everything in between. As I look around I realized I should have thrown in some gardening attire and more cowgirl gear. I'll just need to make do with my three suitcases. OK, I brought five, but can you blame me?

My grandparents are introducing my dad, my stepmom, and Baer to everyone. The mountain of a man is my older second cousin, Junior, they explain. I know Junior usually means small, but in this case I don't even want to know who the senior is. Next, I meet three aunts, four uncles, five cousins, and three second-cousins. After that I sort of lost count. Mountainous Junior keeps looking over at me. You'd think I'd be a bit freaked out after him almost causing me to have a repeat of the cheese puffs incident, but he's not trying to intimidate me, rather keep an eye out for me. Little did I know then just how much he would become my protector.

Everyone helps me carry my cargo into the trailer. As I step inside, I realize it's much bigger on the inside. They don't call it a "double-wide" for nothing! It opens to a small living room with a dining room squeezed off to the side in a back corner. After that is the kitchen, which has every counter filled with boxes and containers of food. Does someone here do catering? It looks like enough to feed an army. For some reason I hear people saying "init" a lot. It must be some type of nickname. My grandfather continues past the kitchen to the narrow hallway in back that holds the bathroom and three bedrooms. The bedrooms may look tiny, but they're each large enough to hold a full bed, a dresser, and a night stand. Thinking about my cavernous room back home in Minnetonka, I'm sort of embarrassed at its excess.

"Apple, here's where you'll stay," my grandfather says as he stops abruptly at the second bedroom. My grandmother shoots him a pensive look.

"Will this be OK? It was your mama's room. We haven't changed it that much. We like the way she decorated it, and everything is still in good condition . . ." My grandma seems to get lost in thought and doesn't finish her sentence. We step inside to lay down my bags. I stop to look at the room. It isn't too big, yet it's cozy with pale purple walls and a quilt in the shape of a star hung on the wall over the bed.

"Of course, I like the room. Thanks," I reply. I can see this room hasn't been used in a while, because there are still remnants of the 1970s and '80s. Which makes sense since my mother hasn't lived here since 1988 when she graduated from high school. At least that's what little my dad told me about her.

Looking around, I realize this room is stuck in a time warp. Now when's the last time you saw an 8-track tape player? Have you forgotten about rotary dial phones? Don't forget the RUSH, ABBA, Duran Duran, and REO Speedwagon posters. It has it all here. There's one term to describe this room: classic 1980s.

Have you ever noticed that you can read a lot about a person by checking out their bedroom? My mom's room has a lot to take in. It's almost too much to think of right now. But I know when I lie down on her bed to go to sleep, I'll be hoping to get to know her more. I've read that objects can take on and retain its owner's aura, or presence. *Please* let that be right.

Everyone leaves me alone to finish unpacking. I put as many clothes as I can into the closets and dresser. I peek under the bed and notice a box filled with what looks like old 8-track music tapes, along with some other cassette tapes, but slide it to the side so I can shove my things under there. 8-track tapes were book-sized music tapes that were all the rage in the 1970s.

It's not that I don't want to go out to visit with all of my relatives. I can hear them with my family in the kitchen. Judy is politely trying to say she really isn't hungry, but thank you anyway for the venison jerky. Mmmmm. Fresh dried deer. Baer, of course, is devouring any and everything offered him. I am so glad I won't be with him in the car again. That could be deadly. Deer and spicy Cheetos leftovers. No thanks.

My Minnetonka family comes in the bedroom and gives the obligatory hugs and goodbyes. Baer asks if I'll be going hunting while I'm here, because the venison jerky is awesome. I inform him that I didn't pack my day-glow orange jumper, so no, I will not be hunting or eating Bambi any time soon.

It's a mixture of relief and sadness when I hear them get in the Land Rover and leave. They were my buffer for a few minutes between my relatives. But I have to make this work.

Chapter 6

I'M LYING ON THE bed, just taking this all in as dusk sets in outside. My eyes are looking at the ceiling and I can just make out some glow-in-the-dark stickers in the shape of constellations. Cool. I love this room. It even *smells* good. Actually, the scent is coming from the open window. What is that smell? It's a mixture of laundry soap, lavender, and oranges.

I decide to try out the bed. After a few minutes, I'm drifting off. I'm in the place just between lucidity and slumber when I hear something.

"Pssssst."

My eyes shoot open faster than you can say "America's Most Wanted."

"Who's there?" I whisper.

"Hey," a faceless voice hisses from the window.

There it is again!

Jumping up, I roll onto the carpet and under the bed. Isn't this ironic? Because under the bed is always the first place the serial killer looks. Always.

The open window produces a loud scratch, then a plink sound. Someone, or something, is coming in! Great. I won't see my family again—either of them—and they'll find me here buried in a pink trailer. Which reminds me. I feel around for the huge 8-track music tapes I saw earlier. Grabbing one, I lob it over my head as I stick my hand out.

It seems to do the trick because the noise has stopped. But what just happened here? Doesn't anyone want to check on me? After what seems like hours, I slip out from under the bed to peer toward the sound of the near-crime.

I was right! Someone, or something, tried to slit the window and open it. I tip-toe over to get a closer look. By the way, I'm sort of hooked on the show *CSI: Crime Scene Investigation* and thought I should possibly look for clues.

Back to the caper at hand. After checking the window scene at my grandparents' trailer (pink) I see the thing that was thrown into my mom's room when I heard that noise. When I bend down to take a closer look, I realize it's a glass jar. Now who would throw a jar in a window? I pick it up, hold it to the light. What's in there? It's dirt. Someone pushed open my window, bent back the screen, and threw a jar of dirt in the room.

What does this mean? Is it a secret code for something on the reservation? Like, "Go home, weirdo? You're a dirt bag?"

There is no way I'm staying in this room any longer by myself, so I quickly walk back out to the living room. I can still see about ten relatives, at least I'm assuming they're relatives, sitting at various places. They all stop and look at me, then glance down at the jar I'm holding.

My grandfather looks up from his recliner and says, "Kekway?" *What*? "What's dat you've got?"

"Someone pushed it in my window."

"Oh, 'zat right?" he asks, looking up from his newspaper.

"They want me to leave," I whisper.

"Who wants to *heave*?" Grandpa yells.

"What? No, somebody doesn't want me here. It's some type of message, or maybe even a threat! They put *dirt* in the jar."

"Now why would anyone put a *shirt* in your car?" he asks.

Right now, the relatives look as if they're watching a tennis match. First looking at me, and then turning when my grandfather speaks.

Apparently, Grandpa is hard of hearing. I say up, he hears cup. You say tree, he hears knee. It's making for some interesting conversations.

"Xavier!" my grandma shouts at Grandpa. "You turn on your hearing aid right now so Apple can talk to you. Go ahead, my girl. Your mooshum forgets to turn up his aid so I have to remind him that he's no spring chicken anymore and his hearing isn't too good, but he's such a dear."

"Oh, no, Marie" Grandpa says to her, "I don't want a beer. Dat woman . . . says da oddest tings at times." The funny thing is he looks sideways at me with upturned corners of his mouth. Then he just sits and rocks in his chair, letting the subtle grin settle down again. When no one is looking, he winks at me, and then does some weird puckering with his lips in Grandma's direction.

I'm not sure exactly, but I wonder if my grandfather is playing my grandma. Making her, and everyone else for that matter, think he can't hear—or at least can't hear better than he lets on. At least I think that's what he meant. I sure hope that lip thing isn't contagious, or worse, hereditary. Drat. At least it gets my mind off of the jar of dirt.

* * *

I'm waiting for everyone in the trailer to go home, but they seem to have other ideas. At my house back with Dad, Judy, and Baer, it's an unwritten rule that guests stay two to four hours, then politely excuse themselves to go do some made-up errand. Not here in Morinville, North Dakota. The relatives are here, and more seem to keep showing up.

As I listen to the conversations floating around me, I pick up what must be an accent of theirs up here on the reservation. It's the way some of the Indians here speak, but not all. I notice that the "th" sound in front of words aren't pronounced, but instead are said like a "d" or sometimes a "t." And when they talk it reminds me of riding a roller coaster. They change their pitch and slowly let their words slide up and down as the sentence continues. It makes me think that their dialect matches the gentle sloping of the land here: up and down, up and down. So much more interesting than the flat Minnesota accent. Ya. Sure. You betcha.

All that food in the kitchen keeps multiplying. If there were seven baskets over-flowing with fish, I'd almost think it was a downright miracle. I guess it's some sort of party. Everyone knows each other and my grandma is trying to introduce me, but after meeting the fortieth or forty-first person, my mind just shuts down and I nod to everyone. Who knew you could cram so many Native Americans into a tiny space? Oh wait, I guess that's what the government did with Indian reservations to begin with. Uncle Sam should be called Uncle Cram.

I wish, for once in my life, I had the ability to flit around and meet and greet people I didn't know. Sad, isn't it, that I wish I could talk to my own relatives? But there's just something inside me that makes it so hard, so painfully difficult to approach people I don't know and actually talk to them.

My whole life, I've always felt like a character in *Star Wars*. Surrounding me wherever I go is a force field. It's an invisible bubble that coats me and when I walk around it keeps people from getting close to me. I can be in a crowded room, like tonight, but there's this force field. When I walk to the left, people shuffle away and conversations stop. When I veer to the right, folks nod politely and make room for the unseen energy they feel as I pass. It's not only a physical separation, but also an emotional one. Have you ever felt that way? That even in a sea of people, whether large or small, no one can really *see* you? You'd think it would be cool to have a super power, to be invisible, but I'd do anything just to be noticed. I wish the force were with me. Help me, Obi-Wan Kenobi. You're my only hope.

My grandmother looks at me across the kitchen with her head tilted to the side and puts a finger to her chin. It looks like she's trying to solve the *New York Times* Sunday edition crossword puzzle.

"Now, my girl, here is your second cousin on your mother's side, Annette. And here is your Great-Uncle Morris. He's Grandpa's uncle on his mother's side. That would be your great-grandma, Elizabeth," she says nodding to this person and that while pulling me to her with a great bear of a hug.

This continues for what seems like forever. The food is set out and it's starting to sink in that everyone is here for me. This is a welcome home party for yours truly. I move out the door and back onto the deck where I see the mountain man, or Junior, as everyone calls him. He looks in my direction and nods slightly. It's just enough of a recognition that my fear of him starts to melt. I don't quite know what to say, but seeing everyone here is starting to overwhelm me. I'm afraid that someone will ask me about my mother. And I'm afraid that no one will say anything about her, either.

I must have a look in my eyes that resembles a caged animal because my grandmother suggests that I go take a walk outside for a few minutes to get some air. What do I do when I'm getting stressed out (besides the foreign exchange student act)? I usually head for a secluded spot, like a closet. But since it's tight corners inside and out on the deck, I find a solitary place in the backyard on the swing.

I don't care how old you are, at any age a swing is a beautiful thing. When you pump your legs and start moving, it's almost as if the wind is darting in and around you caressing your cares away. I continue swinging for about ten minutes, just taking in the scene back at the trailer (I think it's actually a magenta color) and how it is overflowing with people. These people are linked to me, to my blood, through my mother. I should get up there and visit with them, but I just don't know how to yet.

"Do ya want me to push ya?"

I spin around to the voice. "What? Who's there?"

"I just know a lot 'bout swingin'," the voice says. The high-pitched voice seems to be coming from a wooded area in the backyard next to the woodpile.

"OK, here's the deal," I spew to the mystery voice, "I was just dropped off to a family I don't even know! And I'm pretty sure there's someone stalking me and throwing things in my window to get me to go home. So, if you want to say something to me, just show yourself!"

Out from behind a blue spruce walks a little sprite of a girl. She looks to be around five years old with an avalanche of chestnut curls spilling down her back. The little girl just stands there with a tilted head, smiling.

"Well, come on den," she says as she turns around.

I watch her make her way up the steps and into the trailer. The people sitting on the deck pat her head as she walks by. Everyone seems to know her. What in the world kind of place is this?

After letting the swing come to a stop, I search for a glimpse of the slight girl. I can't see her anymore and I've calmed down a bit, so I decide I need to get to the bottom of this. After all, I was almost tonight's main attraction on the latest episode of *America's Most Wanted*. (I had to quit watching that show by myself last year because every time the wind would howl outside the window of our family room I would have a near heart attack, so it's the only time I ask Baer to watch TV with me. If there's someone outside looking in deciding who to kill, I figure my odds are better if there's another person in the room with me. Who better to offer as a sacrifice than your own little brother?)

I make my way up the deck and "Pardon me" and "excuse me" my way through the crowd of relatives. By the time I make it inside, that little girl has parked herself between Junior and my grandmother at the kitchen table. She's eating what looks to be a triangle-shaped donut, with all the crumbs dotting her chin. Now that I'm inside, I can better see this little lass. I noticed her curls out by the swing when she talked to me, and now I can see the rest of her. Her skin has a golden hue that sets off her tan. I can honestly say that those are the prettiest eyes I've ever seen. They look like little caramels under thick eyelashes.

I must have been staring at her, because she turns and, with a full mouth of food, says, "Bang."

"Excuse me?" I utter, amazed.

"Bang? Bullets?" little caramel-eyes says. Little bits of food are spewing out as she tries to talk. It's sort of gross, and a tad violent. Kids are pretty disgusting when they eat. Remind me never to apply for a job as a cafeteria lunch lady.

"Well, what kind of thing is that to say?" I answer, a bit too forceful.

"BANG! BANG! BULLETS!" yells caramel-eyes.

I glance between Junior and my grandmother, looking for some help here. Obviously, this child is prone to violent outbursts. But they don't discipline her, or reprimand her, or step in to help at all. See, that's the problem with kids today. No direction.

As I take a breath to start my lecture on how to be polite and not verbally "shoot" the guest of honor (me), she holds out a small chubby hand with one of the donuts. She smiles — with a mouth full of the bread and what looks like hamburger — and whispers, "bang?"

Grandma gently wipes the little girl's mouth and takes the donut from her outstretched hand and turns to me.

"Apple, I see you've met Little Inez."

"Oh," I answer, "not formally."

"Now, Inez, run along and tell Grandpa that he needs to come and carve the ham," Grandma says as she shoos the child away.

After Inez leaves the kitchen I ask, "Uhh, Grandma, is Little Inez . . . you know . . . a 'special needs' child? Because, well . . . she seems to have a violent streak."

"What *are* you talking about, Apple?" she asks.

Junior almost spits out his food as he says through laughter, "Apple, you *do* know dat Inez was offering you *baeng*. Dat's Indian fry bread in the Turtle Mountain Michif language." He holds up one of the triangle donuts and pops one into his mouth. "As you can see," Junior pats his Buddha-sized belly, "dat's what helps keep me in shape." A rail-thin woman with spiked hair sitting down next to him lets out a great howl.

"Oh, well, OK. That explains the bang part. But she was yelling for bullets. Every city girl knows *that's* a threat!" I shriek.

"My girl," Grandma whispers in my ear, "Inez was offering you a Turtle Mountain food staple, *le bullet* in the Michif language, or bullets." She nods to Junior as he pops a meatball in his mouth.

"So . . . bullets are *meatballs*," I say. "I get it now. But why didn't she just call them what they are?"

At the same time, both Junior and my grandmother chuckle and say, "She did!"

Chapter 7

BY NOW I'M FEELING a little better that some five-year-old isn't trying to kill me. Later Junior lets me know that bullets are meatballs in gravy and are usually served on New Year's Day when families visit each other going house to house saying, "Le Bonne Année!" *Happy New Year!*

Grandma is busy back tending to the ham as Grandpa comes in, sharpening his carving knives. I can hear her tell him to "carve it thin," and he answers something that makes Grandma let out a sigh and shake her head.

My grandpa makes his way over to me.

"Apple," Grandpa tips down to softly say, "What's da matter? You don't look so good."

Do these people remember nothing? "I think I mentioned something about a jar of dirt pushed through the window. What kind of gift is *dirt*? I mean really? Who is trying to make a statement like 'you're a dirt bag,' or is it more like 'you're filthy like dirt?'"

My grandfather smiles to himself and lets me know that I just need to keep this thought for now and worry about making sense of it later. After my little tirades, like I just had, I'm so used to my dad and Judy rolling their eyes and shooing me to my room to calm down. But my grandpa doesn't make a big deal out of it, and none of the people in the house (oops, I mean trailer) even take notice when I just had diarrhea of the mouth.

Since Grandpa isn't giving me any answers, I change the subject and try to learn more about this Little Inez.

"So, Grandpa, if that girl is *Little* Inez, which one of these people is *Big* Inez? Which relative here is her mom?"

Junior looks at Grandpa with a solemn gaze and peers around to see if anyone is listening. He beckons me with his enormous sausage-sized finger to come closer. Junior leans to me and in a low tone says, "Well, see, Little Inez's mom had some problems with drugs. Two years ago, she ran off with some guy she met at da casino. We haven't heard from her since. Every now and den Little Inez gets an envelope in da mail with a few dollars in it. We're guessing it's from Big Inez."

My chest feels like someone threw a lead football into my heart. That poor little girl. I never knew my mom, but this little one had her mother leave her . . . *on purpose.* Could her mom be dead? Should they have started an investigation?

"Well, how do you know her mom isn't dead somewhere?"

Grandfather replies matter-of-factly, "Well, dat's why we all, everyone in da Turtle Mountains, reads obituaries. From coast to coast we have relatives who keep an eye out for Big Inez in dere newspapers. It's a sad way to look for da dead, but for dose on drugs, dere families *are* dead. It's up to da rest of us in Indian country to look out for da orphans. Apple, we may not have fancy houses here, or expensive cars, but da one treasure we *do* have is family. A big, extended, crazy family. Little Nezzie—dat's what we call her—lives with her older sister, Tara, now."

"I understand, Grandpa. But I heard Grandma earlier tell Inez to find 'Grandpa'—you. But if she's not my cousin, how can you be her grandpa?"

Grandpa looks at me and smiles, "Little Nezzie wanted a grandpa and grandma, so she started calling us dat. Your grandma and I answered. See, Apple, in Indian culture, grandparents—and elders—are highly respected. It's a great honor to have lived dis long and to have learned many life lessons, most of dem hard ones. In Indian country, in da Indian way, family is necessary for survival. Many of your relatives dat came here have mixed and blurred da line of what outsiders may understand. See dose two men by da back door? Dey're cousins. Dey may be fourth or second cousins. It may be a loose definition of a cousin, but it doesn't matter to dem. And Junior, here, calls just about everyone on dis reservation "auntie" or "uncle." Even I don't really know da exact family lines of everyone in dis house today, yet it makes it almost better because we're all in da inner circle of close family. Last year, Nezzie started calling us Mooshum and Kookum. *Grandpa* and *Grandma* in the Michif language. And so now, she's our granddaughter, too."

Just as I was asking this my grandmother walks into the kitchen carrying empty dishes and stacking them in the sink. Man, can these people eat. She must have overheard and understood our conversation.

"Let's see . . . Apple, you are Junior's cousin . . . no wait. Technically that's my cousin's child, so it would make you his third cousin. And Big Inez was *my* second cousin, twice removed, so . . . hmmm . . . Let's try this from Mooshum's side, Xavier's side. Now he was Big Inez's auntie's cousin by marriage . . . so Apple, that makes you and

Little Nezzie . . ." Grandma starts counting on her fingers, staring out at everyone.

I try to make some sense of this lineage, "OK, so I get that Junior is some type of cousin. And Big Inez was some sort of cousin . . . removed."

Just then Little Inez glides into the kitchen, wiping her mouth. She stops when she sees me and gives me a smile.

I continue asking how Little Inez and I are related, "So, Grandma, you would be Inez's cousin, and that makes Junior another one of Little Inez's cousins . . ." I contemplate the connection as I point between Little Inez and myself, "So what does that make me?"

"Lucky," Little Nezzie says, without losing a beat.

She brings the house down.

* * *

Later that evening after most people left (yes, it took a while), I could feel exhaustion set in. A few people were helping clean up in the kitchen with my grandma and she tells me not to worry about helping, to just go to bed.

I need to do something to help clean up, to show my appreciation. That little lecture that my dad is always yelling (ever so politely) keeps popping up in my head. It's the lecture about how you're supposed to show people your thanks by doing something nice in return. Apparently, I didn't understand him completely when he first told me this.

Judy was making a new recipe for chocolate pudding. She was trying to use up a box of some old ingredients (first clue something was amiss) and didn't check the expiration date. Baer *loves* anything chocolate, so he was the first one to dig in. Since it smelled pretty good I grabbed a spoon and dug in, too. I looked at my almost finished bowl and the pudding was *moving*! Maggots—they're not just for breakfast anymore.

"Move!" I yelled as I reached for the garbage can and yacked into it. I threw up, making sure not to get any of my puke on the floor. One nice thing deserves another. Dad's right. Paying back is a good quality to live by.

Hmmm . . . I never noticed it before, but our family seems to have a lot of vomit stories. I guess some families have game night. We heave together. The family that throws up together, grows up together . . . or something like that.

Back to doing something to show my appreciation for my party. I grab two full garbage bags from the pile next to the sink and head out to the garbage cans I saw out back. Walking through the thinning crowd of relatives, I nod to this one and say goodnight to another one. Most of the older people here pat my arm or touch my hand, and always add "my girl" when they're talking to me. But they also say it to Little Nezzie, too. Not quite sure what that's all about.

Just as I get to the garbage cans out back, I try to walk around a man. He's lighting a cigarette, and doesn't seem to get the idea that maybe he could move out of my way so I can get rid of these bags that are starting to rip and are sending melting ice cream down my arms.

This guy standing in front of me reminds me of pictures of the Marlboro Man: tall, tan, and wearing cowboy boots and a hat.

"So, *you're* Apple. I knew your ma. She was a real beauty."

"Oh, well, thanks I guess," I say, shocked that this man could be old enough to have known my mother. He is tall, over 6'5", with short spiky black hair. Looking at his sculpted face with high cheekbones and dark pools for eyes, I blush a bit. Then he speaks again.

"But you don't look nothin' like her," he says, glancing at me from head to toe.

"And who are you? I've met so many relatives today, I just can't seem to keep all the names straight," I say apologetically.

He squints as he looks at me, then his eyes look over my shoulder to the trailer as he says, "I'm Karl. I lived next to your ma growin' up. Saw you talking to that little Inez girl earlier."

Laughing I reply, "Yeah, that little girl sure is something!"

"Oh, she's something all right. Her ma ran out on her. Left with some white guy. Best you stay away from that girl. Nothing but trouble comes from mixing with *les blancs*, from *whites*," Karl says as he blows smoke in my face and takes two steps toward me, never taking his eyes off me. Pretty sure this Karl fellow isn't aware of the second-hand smoke studies.

Not quite sure what to say, I try walking around him to attempt to put the garbage away.

Stepping in front of me, he gets down in my face, "Your ma and I spent some time together, but then she left for college and got too *good* for us. Heard she married a rich *white* guy and had you. White guys think they can swoop in and take the best of our Indian women." Karl stops to take a drag of his cigarette. He's not looking *at* me, so much as looking *through* me.

Stepping so close to me that I could see the pupils of his stormy eyes, he whispers, "And what kind of name is *Apple*? Why, do you know what kind of Indians we call 'Apple' — " Karl was cut short from finishing.

"Hey, Karl!" Junior yells, walking and waving maniacally as he bounds down the deck steps at full speed. "You got da early shift tomorrow at work, man. Best you be getting home. I'll give you a ride."

Karl is surprised at how quickly Junior is beside him and is visibly shaken. "Oh, no thanks. I can stay and catch a ride with my uncle—"

"No problem at all. I'm going right by your house." Junior officially ends the discussion while he grabs the garbage bags and slams them into the cans. Karl jumps from the clamor, both men staring at the other.

Junior continues to rescue me. "Apple, you had a tiring day. Go on in and I'll finish up out here," he booms while looking at Karl.

It seems like a good time to get back inside, so I hand Junior the garbage. There's something about that Karl. An anger floating barely under the surface, just simmering. Being in the middle is usually an annoyance. But this time, being in the middle of these two men, I'm anxious more than I have ever been before to get out of here. And get out of here fast, which is exactly what I did. This wouldn't be the last time—only I didn't know it yet—that Junior would come to my rescue.

Chapter 8

STILL A BIT SHAKEN, I walk back inside and down the short hallway to the bedrooms and glance at the wall. My heartbeat is settling into a slower pace after the backyard encounter. Why did that Karl guy totally freak out on me? And what's he got against having money? Steadying my breathing, I look back up at the wall. And instantly my heartbeat calms down even more. Now why didn't I notice that before? There must be over a hundred pictures covering the corridor paneling. Some pictures are black and white with the edges curling. But I notice only one face. One face I've seen only in my dreams. My mother.

I've been so busy my first day here that I haven't had time to look for her. My eyes travel from frame to frame, searching out my mother. I can see her at her high school graduation. She is more than beautiful. The first thing I see are her midnight eyes, set wide, with cheek bones jutting out from her slim face. Those eyes sing through the picture, and I can almost hear them. Her long wavy hair fights to stay controlled under her graduation cap as she holds onto it with one hand. Her other hand is linked with a shorter girl with a shock of red curls—almost like this other girl's hair was ablaze. What expression does my mom have on her face? In this photo both girls are smiling and laughing at the camera, as if they know the joke and the rest of us are still waiting for the punch line. The story of my life.

I see a faded photo of her as a child, hung up toward the ceiling. She is wearing a white dress with a veil and is standing next to an altar. This must have been her first communion. Either that or she was a child bride. Even at the age of seven or eight years old, she has that same expression that was in the high school portrait. It's not quite smiling eyes, but not laughter either. When I look closer at it, I can see a faint dash of a dimple on her left cheek. Would I have been able to make her that happy had she lived?

This is the most time I've ever spent with my mother, and she's doing a lot of talking.

As I continue looking for pictures of her, I come across some of Grandma and Grandpa when they were younger. I see a lot of Grandpa playing sports, basketball in particular. And there must be three or four pictures of Grandma raising her hand to hide herself as someone tries to capture her on film. The more I rest my eyes on this hallway collage, I see the stark difference between my professional family portraits back home where we're all sitting, poised and practiced and ready for the camera. But all of these photos on the wall hold different images. Here the photographer is a family member capturing laughter. I don't have that in any pictures at home. There, back in Minnesota with Dad, Judy, and Baer, we're practicing for life. Here, in these simple pictures, everyone is *living life*—not just stopping and posing for the camera.

I can feel an arm surround me as I'm moving down the wall, my eyes still searching.

"My girl, you're still up?" my grandmother asks.

"I am; I got caught here looking at your family."

"Eh bien, *well*, they're *your* family, too, Apple!" she whispers.

"I guess you're right, but I just wish I knew my mom. She looks so beautiful . . . and content."

"Come on, let's get you to bed. It's been a long day for you, and we've got a lot to do tomorrow," Grandma says.

We walk together, her with an arm around me, down to my bedroom. I stop when I see a picture of a couple on their wedding day. I recognize Grandpa—and I must say, my grandmother as a young bride was a stunner back in the day.

"Wow, Grandma, you sure are beautiful in your wedding picture."

As she winks at me, she says, "You know what they say, pictures *never* lie."

I lie in bed that night thinking about the day, especially the conversation with Grandpa about who is related to whom. I'm so used to straight and simple answers. This is what I know— direct line of who belongs where: Judy is my stepmom and Baer is my stepbrother. Yet it's sort of nice to not have to put a "step" in front of anyone's name here. When you don't have to step up to a stepmom, and step down to a stepbrother, you can just be on the same level as everyone. A family.

With all this floating around in my mind, it's a miracle I fell asleep. Yes, I may have even drooled on the pillow a bit, but I had a crazy day. I mean really! Think about it: my very white family met some Indians for the first time. Sort of like Columbus's first encounter with the Natives. Only this time it was an uptight white family meeting a mountain-sized Native with an awesome Aussie accent. And this time we can't say that the whites "discovered" anything since the Aussies were here first! (Er, wait, that's not right either.) And *this* time the whites actually left the Natives where they were.

That night there's no problem falling asleep. And I dream. In my dream, I'm walking alone in the woods, calmness contained in the lush landscape. But the tranquility is broken as I turn to follow sounds. I spot a miniature nest caught between a tangle of trailing branches. I can see a tiny baby robin with its indigo blue egg cracked and set aside. This little thing is making all the ruckus? But then I look closer at the nest. Intermixed with twigs and grasses are black threads woven throughout. I reach slowly, tentatively and deliberately, to touch the nest, especially the black string. My fingers are within inches of it, and as my eyes draw nearer, I get a closer look and notice that those aren't pieces of black thread; they're strands of raven-black hair. Could it be from . . .?

As soon as I almost touch the hair, out of the corner of my eye I see someone waving at me. Three young people are swimming in a shallow pond to my left. They're spraying and teasing one another. One of them is beckoning me with a head tilt and subtle hand motion. But as soon as I can get closer for a peek at the face, whoever it is turns back to the group of friends. They look so right, here in my dream. Carefree, happy, and something else . . . they look like they belong. The setting is so serene, as if they have no cares in the world but to wipe away the day's heat and solitude.

Come on. Even in my dreams I'm an outsider? How unfair is that?

Sometimes I think that the only way those who are in the next life have any possibilities to contact us in this life is to do it when we're unconscious or sleeping. We all have our iPods in our ears, the radio on constant scan mode searching for the next song, our text messages flowing heavier than the Nile in the rainy season. Not to mention constantly checking our email or seeing if anyone on Facebook has friended us lately. No wonder God made our bodies need sleep. After spending sixteen hours with our frenetic life, He just needs to knock us out to get a word in edgewise.

How do I find out if this means something? Does this dream mean anything? Do dreams ever mean something?

Who was beckoning to me in my dream? Because I'm not much of a swimmer. It takes forever to do my hair, and when it gets wet it looks like a Brillo pad on caffeine. Really, with all of my issues in life, you'd think the goddess of hair would have been generous. After all, isn't a woman's crowning glory her hair?

* * *

I awaken the next dawn in a puddle of drool the size of Lake Superior. For a second, I can't for the life of me figure out where I am. But then I see Leif. Leif Garret? And Duran Duran? Remember them? You don't? The poster on the wall next to my bed holds the classic pop icons — feathered hair and all. Coaxing my eyes open the rest of the way proves to be labor intensive. Yet as soon as I realize I'm in the shrine to all things retro, my eyes and body jolt awake. Mom's room. Oh Leif, if only we were born in the same decade. It could have been beautiful. Although, if you ask me, he's a bit too skinny for my taste. Speaking of taste, what is that smell? My stomach insists that I go and explore the aroma.

I throw on some sweatpants and a shirt. It's pretty early, only 5:30 a.m., but I can hear someone banging around in the kitchen. You might think it's odd for a teenager to be up at dawn, but I've always been that way. If there is a sliver of morning light that steals into my bedroom and it hits my eyelids, forget about it. I'm up and I stay up. Now don't go thinking I like getting up this early. Contrary to popular belief, I don't think it's the best time of the day. Nobody in my family is even remotely conscious at this time. So, it's a lonely time of the day because, once again, my companions are me, myself, and I. Even my body can't be a normal teenager.

Chapter 9

I WONDER WHAT MY grandmother is making (quite loudly, I might add) so early this morning. I can hear music floating down the hallway but can't quite make out the tune. As I walk past the hallway photo gallery, I step into the kitchen and hear a loud thud! It sounds as if someone is falling, repeatedly.

I rush to see what the commotion is. And what a commotion it is. There, with a flour-sack dishcloth tied around his waist, is my grandfather, standing over the stove flipping pancakes up into the air. The sound, which I thought was someone falling, is him doing some type of hopping dance step in between the pancake flip and the catch. Move over Baryshnikov — Grandpa's in the house.

"Ah, good morning! How many pan-a-cakes do you want?"

"Wow, they smell amazing! Where's Grandma?" I ask, looking around his shoulder to see what he put in the batter.

"Kekway, *what!* You don't tink your mooshum can cook?"

"Well, I guess I'm just not used to seeing a man cook. Where did you learn to do this?" I can hear Mooshum's Michif accent come through as he replaces a "t" for the "th" in think. Or am I the one with the accent because I use "th?" Doesn't *everyone* have an accent, depending on who is listening?

"Courtesy of da US Army. I was on KP duty a few months during World War II when I was stationed in Poland. I learned dat after a day's worth of fighting, all any soldier wants is a hot meal dat reminds him of home. It may have only taken dem a few minutes to wolf down a meal, but for dose precious moments soldiers were home sitting at dere mama's table. Food does dat to you," Grandpa explains as he points his spatula toward the mountainous stack of pancakes.

"Sounds good to me. Load me up!"

"Now dat's what I like to see. A girl wit an appetite. Now take some bacon and toast, too. Eat up, my girl. You *gotta* eat!"

I gratefully fill my plate, but then turn again to the chef du jour. "Grandpa, what were you doing while you were cooking. The little hop thing?"

"Well, it's called a jig. Red River Jig to be exact. I have my little radio here by da stove, and when it gets to playing old time music, my feet have a mind of dere own. We Michifs like to dance," he adds with a wink.

"Grandpa, I thought Michif was the language up here, not the people. That mixture between French, Cree, a bit of Scottish and Ojibwe?"

"Eya, *yes*, but for some reason we Turtle Mountain people started calling ourselves Michif, too."

Hmmm, someone related to me up at the crack of dawn and dancing what looks like a Scottish jig while making breakfast? It might sound odd, but to me, I totally get it. His feet obeying the music is like when I have to ask those weird questions (which, surprisingly, I haven't had an itch to do here . . . yet).

We Michifs gots to do what we gots to do.

After serving myself a serious second helping of pancakes, I take some toast and bacon. I see some small blueberries and add a heaping pile to my plate. Can I just say, yum? Who knew an elderly man in his sixties could cook like this. And these blueberries? They might possibly be the best I've ever tasted.

"Grandpa, where did you guys buy these blueberries? They're amazing! Would you mind if I run out and buy some more? I just ate the last of them."

"Oh, you like dose berries, do you? Apple, dose were your mama's favorites. Dey're juneberries. When Grandma gets up we'll head out to get some more."

The mention of my mother makes my eyes descend to my plate. My whole life, it's been an unspoken rule that my mother is not talked about in casual conversation. But here, my mother is talked about like she's just left the room and will be back shortly. As if she's still part of the family. I'm beginning to like that.

"Grandpa, what was my mom like when she was growing up?" My eyes are cast down, not wanting to see any pain. But I'm hoping for a glimpse, a new chapter in my life.

When I ask this his entire face changes like a new bud opening on a flower. "Your mama? Well, she was a gift. She sure was. Dere was just so much love in her . . ." He starts to get a faraway look. "But, boy, was she a handful growing up! Ha! We lived out in Flandreau, South Dakota, when she was little. I was finishing my schooling, college, and your grandma worked in a laundry mat. Since we were both working so much we had to hire a babysitter to watch her during da day."

Shaking his head with a laugh that starts in his chest, he adds, "Ha! If only we could *keep* a sitter. We must have gone trough six or seven women in just two months' time."

"OK, so why did they keep leaving?"

Grandpa puts down the dishes he was drying, untucks the towel from his belt and sits next to me at the table. With his fingers he starts counting: "Babysitter number one left after she found your mother trying to clean da kitchen floor. She poured vegetable oil all over, invited our little neighbor girl over, and dey had what looked like a skating party. Feet gliding all over da floor. Babysitter number two quit after realizing dere was a sticky mess by her gas cap on her car. Apparently, *you-know-who* tought da car looked hungry, so she poured grape jelly in da gas compartment. I haven't tought about dis in a long time. Do you want to hear more?"

"Please. I don't know much of anything about her, and when I hear everyone talk about her here, I start to feel . . . I don't know. Lighter."

"I know just what you mean, Apple. Just what you mean. OK, let's see now, where was I? Number tree babysitter quit after she came down with da worst case of poison ivy I've ever seen."

"But how was that Mom's fault?" I ask.

"It seems dat your mom gave the sitter some flowers she picked. And dey just happened to be poison ivy and itching clover. Da rest of da ladies all left for similar reasons," he says shaking his head, with a trace of a smile dancing on his lips. "Which is why your mama's grandma, Elizabeth, started babysitting her. No one else could handle her!"

After thinking for a few minutes (and polishing off the last of the bacon), I have a thought, "But it seems to me that Mom wasn't naughty or bad. She was trying to be helpful. She tried to help clean the floors, make the car 'feel' better, and gave someone flowers. For a young girl, she tried to be helpful in her own way. How is that bad?"

Grandpa smiles a great grin, pats the top of my head, and says, "You know, I tink you just might be right. Ah, I can hear Grandma getting up. We'll go get you some of dose berries you like so much. 'Cause, my girl, you gotta eat!" He's always saying "we gotta eat," but what do I eat to feed my starving soul?

Grandma gets up and chides Grandpa for making a mess in her kitchen, but then hears that I'd like some more juneberries and relents. I'm wondering what I should wear. I mean, I don't want to stand out and make everyone realize I don't fit in, yet I also want to make an impression. What would it feel like to be the same as them? After all, no one around here knows me, and therefore, there's a possibility that I could belong. It's really all I want for Christmas.

Chapter 10

SO, WHAT TO WEAR to a small-town grocery store? I finally decide to go with my favorite denim blue pumps, with the simple jeans and my favorite Abercrombie t-shirt. It is screaming the "down home girl" look. Why am I hearing Cher's "Cherokee People" song in my mind?

"Xavier, didn't you tell your granddaughter where you're going to get the berries?"

Grandpa's lips start to curl upwards as he looks sideways at us, "Now, why would I do dat, Marie?"

"Eh bien. Well, Apple, didn't he tell you where juneberries come from?" Grandma asked. I love it when she says "eh bien." It comes out sounding like *uh baaaaa*. It's French, but with a Turtle Mountain twist. Like a croissant, but on a stick. A croissant-cicle.

And with that, my grandparents start laughing. The only thing is, once again, I don't know the punch line. Yet, those juneberries really are good. So, let's get a move on!

There's a knock on the front door. Junior walks in the house just then and, with his arms spread wide, says, "Da great chief has arrived!" Then he moves his arms and hips to imaginary hula music. There's just something about Junior that makes you love him. He kisses Grandma on the cheek and takes a sip of her coffee.

"Heard you're lookin' for berries. Let's roll."

Junior, Grandpa, and I get into the truck and head out. We pass one and then another small-town grocery store, but we keep going.

"Ah, Grandpa, what store are we heading toward? I'm sort of getting hungry again, and you've passed all the stores."

"City girl," Junior says, shaking his head and laughing.

We pull off the road onto a jumble of overgrown bushes and lumbering trees overhead. They both start to get out, then walk to the back of the truck and grab two metal pails and a plastic bag. As I try to get out and follow them, the heels of my expensive shoes sink into the ground. Step by step, I have to extract my shoes after each humiliating tread, and then my left heel snaps right off.

It seems that you can't buy juneberries. Oh no, that would be too simple. We have to drive to this remote location and search for the elusive berries. In the woods. With all the bugs. And animals. Please say there aren't ticks here. Yet, those juneberries really are good. So, let's get a move on!

Under my breath I say, "I wear these $300 shoes out here looking for *berries*? I assumed there was some type of civilization around here . . . $300!"

"What's da matter?" they all ask simultaneously.

"This!" I yell as I hold up and point to my shoes. "Bloomingdales . . . $300!"

My grandfather—with that devilish grin, stopping and holding up his worn cowboy boots—points and says, "Kmart, $16." As he says this, he throws me the plastic bag he was carrying. Inside is another pair of soft brown cowboy boots (Kmart, no doubt), just my size. I slink down and switch shoes. He looks back at me and winks. I guess it is kind of funny. And these boots fit me like a glove.

After I follow them for twenty minutes, we find a spot surrounded with juneberry bushes. I think I just may have found heaven. It's like regular nature out here. But after an hour and a half of picking, I'm getting famished!

I turn to Junior and ask, "When do we go back for lunch?"

And he does the oddest thing. He puckers up his lips and looks past me. Huh?

I ask again, "Uh, hello, shouldn't we be getting back to eat lunch? I'm getting hungry."

Oh. My. Gosh. He's doing it again! That thing with the smootchie lips. I ask a simple question, "Junior, where's the cooler so we can eat lunch? I'm starved." So, what does he do? Puckers his lips as he turns his face slightly, and then looks back at me.

What to do? I look around, not sure what to say (is he having a mental lapse?). I ask again, "Junior, did you bring something for us to eat?" There, he's at it again. Does anyone know CPR, because I'm thinking lip puckering is a definite sign of a stroke?

I'm getting freaked out by his behavior, now. We're too far out in the woods (or as they call it: the bush) for me to call for help. I ask again louder, "Hello! Where's the food?" Yep, you guessed it. Junior's reaction is the puckering-lips-while-turning-your-head response.

After I stare at him for a few more seconds, he says, "Apple, I'm a little worried 'bout you. What is it you don't understand? Dere's lunch," he says, as his chubby fingers touch the wild juneberry bushes.

"So why didn't you just say that?" I ask.

"I did tell you where lunch is." And he puckers his lips as he looks at the closest juneberry bush. Smiling, he adds, "Lips make a good Indian pointer stick." And with that, he puckers and purses his lips towards the juneberries. "Apple, you don't always need words. Be quiet and listen to find da answer you're lookin' for." As he walks away, he lets out a huge fart — to emphasize his point, I guess.

Wow. I am SO out of my element here. I yell over to my grandpa, who's setting up a picnic blanket, "Grandpa, do you want some berries?"

He stops, looks up at the trees and replies, "No. Dey don't look too hairy."

O.M.G. Toto, we're not in Minneapolis anymore.

* * *

After the foray into the depths of the wilderness, Grandpa tells me that I should just hold onto the boots for a while. They are the most comfortable shoes I've ever worn, because someone already did the breaking in. I didn't notice it out in the bush, but now I can see there's a small row of turquoise beads that was hand sewn down the sides and around the foot. I'd say it was Kmart bohemian. And it works.

When we get back home, we all empty out our berry buckets and start washing them in the kitchen. It's quite a haul — four full pails of exquisite luscious juneberries.

"Later, my girl," Grandma says, giving me a hug, "we'll make some pies with them. But for now, go rest for a while. The bush sometimes steals your energy and uses it to replenish the food we take from it."

Before I head back to my bedroom, I turn and ask, "Grandma, I notice you and Grandpa call me 'my girl,' which I get since I'm your granddaughter, but I hear other people up here saying it to me, too. Does it mean I'm sort of adopted by everyone up here?"

Grandma stops and cradles my face between her hands, answering, "It's sort of an endearment. Like how the Southern people call everyone 'dear,' or 'honey.' Do you understand?"

I nod.

"Apple, we're all related somehow, and it's our way of showing that. All of the elders are in charge of raising the children. We believe it, and we treasure our little ones. It comes out so naturally that I don't even think we know it."

"Do you say it only to girls?"

Grandma stops to think, "Well, no, we say 'my boy,' too." And with that she kisses me again and points me in the direction of the bedroom.

Why does it seem as if I'm sleeping so much here? I leave the bedroom window open to capture some of the warm breeze. As I drift off to sleep, I gently tug the blanket towards my chin. I never noticed the pattern on it. It's a giant star made up of tiny multi-colored triangles. Before I know it, I'm dreaming again. It's the same dream again. In the woods with the nest and the water.

Bam! What in the world? I'm yanked from my dream by an object that lands smack dab in the middle of my forehead. Ahhh! Why do I keep having this dream? What is this thing that settled on my forehead?

Cross-eyed, I grab what seems to be a baggie filled with who knows what from my head and sit up. The sun has thrown away the shadows, and my room is filled with daylight. Before taking a closer look, I see that the window screen next to my bed has a fresh tear in it. Grandpa fixed it late last night. I tried to tell him about the miracles of duct tape and how it would solve that pesky torn screen, but no, he wanted to fix it right he said. If duct tape is wrong, I don't want to be right.

As I turn the baggie over, I can see that it's filled with some type of weed. I pull a small handful out and look closer at its silvery green leaves, similar looking to miniature oak leaves, clinging to the stem. Great. So, first there was a jar of dirt thrown at me. And now some weeds chucked in my room, too. Disgusted, I shove the weeds back into the baggie and start to zip it up—and while doing so, some of the leaves got crushed. Oh. Oh wow.

As soon as I crush the leaves they emit a scent crossed between lavender and pine needles. I yank open the bag to grab the plants and inhale again. That's part of the scent up here in the Turtle Mountains! I first noticed it the minute I stepped out of the Land Rover, and then again when we went just this morning to pick juneberries. Whatever it is, the best perfume from Paris has nothing on this.

It was then that I saw something outside of the window, just next to the gate out back by the alley—and that I hear the rumble of a truck drive past. I can see inside, and Karl is the driver. Did he drop that bag of weeds in my window? And if so, what is he trying to tell me? Is this a warning?

Chapter 11

I HEAD OUT TO the kitchen to see if I can get any answers about the bag of weeds. I thought my life in Minneapolis was odd. This is proving to be to be my own little CSI episode.

Walking out of my bedroom, I peek down the hall to see if anyone is up. I can hear the radio on in the kitchen, so I head that way. As I pass the wall of pictures, I slow down to glance at the pictures of my mother. I can see more photos that I missed that first day. There's a black and white one of her pulling a little dog in a sled. Next to it is a basketball team picture — The Morinville Warriors. Cool. Was my mom a jock? And why didn't I get that gene? Thanks, Dad.

"Well, look who's up! Did you rest well, Apple?" Grandma peeks out from the kitchen. She has her apron on — a type I've never seen before. Back home Judy always has the latest Williams-Sonoma patterned apron, but Grandma's looks more like a snap-front smock. It suits her. I like it. I wonder if it comes in French blue. That color tends to take notice away from my dark tan, which seems to be getting worse up here. Apparently, they don't believe in sunscreen. And yet . . . everyone's skin sort of looks like mine. Or I guess, my skin is looking like everyone's.

"Yeah, thanks. I really feel like I got a good rest . . . except . . ." I hesitate to bring up the dream and the pummeling of weeds. It's bad enough that I have one family that rolls their eyes at me whenever I bring up my issues. I don't need everyone up here to jump on that bandwagon, too.

"Oh," Grandpa asks as he walks in from the living room, "what's going on? Is da bedroom not working for you? It was your mom's. We tought you'd like to stay in dere. Maybe it's too much for now."

"No! I love it. It's just that . . . well . . ."

Grandma comes next to me at the table, gently rubs my back, "Now you just tell us what's wrong. I could always tell when your mama was upset. Such a dear thing. Never in a million years would she tell us when something was bothering her, but there was a look in her eyes and a sorrow woven throughout her voice. Apple, you have that same feeling about you now."

"Well, OK. First, there's this," I say as I take the bag of sweet smelling weeds from my pocket. "Wait a minute. Do you think this is some type of illegal substance? I think I've heard that marijuana has a sweet smell. Could someone have tried to plant drugs on me? And they're going to call the DEA (the Drug Enforcement Agency, for you innocent types) and have me taken out of here in handcuffs? I'm too delicate for the slammer! I wouldn't last a day!"

Before I can finish my psychotic rant, my grandmother chimes in, "Oh, well it looks like you've found some Turtle Mountain sage. Doesn't that just smell wonderful? Where did you pick that? We used to have a patch out back by the swing, but lately someone's been picking it as soon as it grows back."

"Sage? This is sage. Oh, well, OK . . . but *I* didn't pick it. It was thrown in my window again. Do you think it's that Karl, or some serial killer?"

Apparently, I've said something comical because my grandparents look at me, then to each other, and start to crack up.

"Why, my girl, sage is considered medicine to Indian people. A gift, not a drug," Grandpa says.

"A gift? These could be warnings!" I say incredulously. "A jar of dirt and a bag of some green weeds are somehow gifts? Remind me to never invite them to my batmitzva."

"My girl, you do know you're not Jewish, don't you?" Grandma asks, worried.

"Well, of course, I'm not Jewish, but what type of voodoo priest offerings is this person giving me? I once read about the Aztec religion. Let's see . . . was it Montezuma? Anyway, they greeted Cortez's army generals with a grand welcoming feast, and before anyone grabbed the first potato olé, Montezuma's priests sprinkled human blood over the food. Human blood!" I spew.

"Enough!" Grandpa says. "You must remember dat here, Native people may not have money to buy fancy gifts of clothes or jewelry. What dey have is demselves. We give our time and our talents, which is more precious dan gold because we give of our selves; we give of our body, mind, and spirit. So, we don't know what dese are, gifts or threats. Just hold tight, my girl."

The tenacity of his loyalty quiets my tirade. I slink down into my seat and am humbled by his explanation. Up here, in the Turtle Mountains, they don't seem to get worried about too much.

In an inaudible whisper, I say "I am so sorry. This is not an excuse, but when I have a thought in my mind, I just spew it out. The last thing I want is to hurt you, Grandpa. You and Grandma are, well, all that I have up here. I just can't tell if someone is trying to warn me, threaten me, or what with these things I keep finding. What if it's . . . that Karl, right outside my window— "

Grandma cuts me off and puts her arms around me giving me a squeeze worthy of a sumo wrestler at dinner time. They both leave me alone with my thoughts, along with the jar of dirt and bag of weeds—I mean sage. I decide to start a little "collection" on top of my dresser. I lie down on my bed and just stare at them. Why on earth is someone giving me these? The sage, I can understand. It just smells good. But the jar of dirt? Come on.

Lord, everything is getting weird up here. But I'm kinda starting to fit in. At least they listen to me. Who knew that I just needed to find the oddest people I have ever met to finally fit in? Like they say, truth is stranger than fiction. And this Indian family and reservation is strange personified, with me center ring.

After just embarrassing myself (what's new), I decide to make some toast and am about to smear butter on it when Grandma looks at me, then puckers her lips. I know *now* that she's not having a stroke, but just pointing at something. But what?

"Uh, Grandma? I'm sort of new to the silent lip pointer; could you help me out a bit?"

Oh no, of course she doesn't. With a glint in her eye, she just smootchie-points and grins at something on the table. There's a tub of what looks like margarine on the table. I'm no cook, but I know when something looks good. It seems Grandma is hinting at this tub of tan guck. On the outside it says "Imperial Cinnamon Spread," and on the inside is pure heaven. Wow! I put some of that on my toast, and if there was a spirit of spreads this would be it.

"Thanks, Grandma. This was awesome. I think I'll go get ready for the day now."

"Just a minute, my girl. Feel free to look around your mama's room. I never knew why I was keeping it intact, not changing anything over the years. But now I know . . . we were waiting for you. It's yours now."

She kisses me on top of my head and holds my face in her hands as she whispers, "My, you're so much like her. That hair of yours just won't listen to anything your brush tries to tell it, does it? And your eyes. I can look in them and almost hear your mama's laughter. Go on, my girl, get ready."

I give her the biggest hug. How can anyone be so nice? She makes me feel as if I'm the most important person in her life. And I've just met her this summer! Is that what my mom was like? There's one last thing nagging the narrows of my mind.

"Grandma, do you ever have weird dreams?" I ask.

"Well, let's see," she looks up and wistfully answers, "there was that dream I had when I won the 'Showcase Showdown' and Bob Barker gave me a kiss on the cheek."

Grandma lets out a chuckle and adds, "But I don't think that's what you mean. What's troubling you, Apple?"

"Well, I keep having the same dream since I've been here. And it just keeps me thinking . . ." I trail off.

Grandma nods inquisitively, "Keeps you thinking about what, Apple? Now don't be ashamed or embarrassed. When we dream, it could be a silly nighttime escapade that means nothing. Or — "

Excited I cut in, "Or? Or what? Do you think that dreams mean something?"

Touching my cheeks gently she says, "Remember to let others finish their thoughts. We were given two ears and only one mouth, which means we should listen twice as much as we speak. If you listen, Apple, you may just hear the answer to your heart's question."

"I'm sorry, Grandma. My mouth just can't seem to sync with my brain. Please, go on."

"Well, Apple, I think you have a dream you are wondering about, hmmm?"

A wave of relief washes my soul. Someone doesn't think I'm crazy! "So, here's my dream. Can you tell me what it represents? So, in the dream — "

But before I can describe anything, she cuts me off as she holds up a hand, "Oh, no. I don't know anything about interpreting dreams. But I think we should go visit your Auntie Auber. I know pies, I know playing BINGO, but I don't know the first thing about interpreting dreams. Your Auntie Auber has a gift. She really is quite something."

"So, this Auntie Over — " I start to ask, but am cut off again.

"No, No! Not Over, Auntie Auber, rhymes with clover. It's short for Aubergine."

Like that clears anything up. This family has some odd names. A few days ago at my welcome home party I think I even heard someone talking to someone named King, and then there was KoKo, and even a Browner, and a lot of people called "Init." Hasn't anyone around here heard of Dick and Jane? But this is coming from me, Apple.

Grandma keeps looking at me, like I should have made some type of connection to Auntie Aubergine. But there is no bell ringing in my head.

She looks at me and turns her head saying, "You know, *aubergine*, as in eggplant!"

"Umm, Grandma . . . I have no idea what you're saying." Should I be worried about her? What are the signs of dementia? Is it red sky at night sailor's delight? Wait, wrong wives' tale.

After I don't reply, my grandmother sighs and then with outstretched hands explains, "Auntie Aubergine is named after the French word for eggplant. Eggplants are purple." She looks at me to make sure I'm taking this all in without sarcasm. "Aubergine's father was a Frenchman who married a beautiful Turtle Mountain Chippewa girl who had eyes the color of woodland violets. I think he married her because she reminded him of home. You see, his family came from a long line of famous cultivators of lavender—the finest French lavender you've ever had the privilege to smell. Remember we told you that the French have always mingled with our people from the days of the fur traders and trappers? No one can resist a Turtle Mountain girl." She winks to prove her point. And wiggles her hips a bit, too.

"Well, Aubergine's father, François, was so excited to be blessed with a child, that when he saw the baby and looked into her purple eyes, he saw the hues of his childhood. When it came time to name Auntie Auber, her father—remembering his beloved and adored lavender—asked that her name somehow honor that purple shade. And was able to convince his wife to name her Aubergine."

I hesitate before asking this question, "So why didn't he just name her Violet?"

Grandma looks at me, thought about what I said, and let out a hearty laugh.

"Well, my girl, I never thought about it that way. He could have, I guess. But he chose to name his daughter a color that was prevalent in his childhood. And since we can't grow lavender in this cold North Dakota climate, he chose the next best thing — eggplant. The garden vegetable that tinted his childhood and then his future."

"So, I, Apple, have an Aunt Eggplant?" If someone wrote this, it couldn't have been odder. But I have another question, "Grandma, you said 'Chippewa,' but I thought we were Michif, which is part Ojibwe?"

"Eya, yes, some say Chippewa, some Ojibwe, and some even say Anishinaabe, but it's basically all about tribal origins. Along the way the names got twisted, white people got confused and different names came out on treaties and such. These names just stuck, I guess."

Yep, we're your garden variety oddballs. And with an aunt named after an eggplant, you'd think I would be horrified. Well, you'd be wrong. My whole life I've been an oddball. Always popping between two worlds, and now up here in the Turtle Mountains I'm feeling like there's something of me up here. I'm not such a side show attraction stuck in the middle. Up here I'm part of the circus. It's good to begin to belong.

But come on, eggplant? At least I'm named after something that tastes good.

Chapter 12

BEFORE GRANDPA COMES INTO the room, I can smell his after-shave enter the kitchen. It's a woodsy smell. Sort of like a pile of pine boughs after a spring thunderstorm — strong, yet simple.

"Did I hear someone say Auntie Auber? Oh, no. I . . . I tink I had better go on up to da old place to check on da ponies," he says, trying not to make eye contact with his wife.

From the few days I've been here, I've learned that "the old place" is the forty acres Grandpa owns. It's his childhood land where he grew up and a place he spends a lot of time. He told me that there is a horse up there just dying to meet me. I may have to check that out. I do have cowboy boots now, ya know. Yee-haw!

But right now, forty acres of land sounds to me like the perfect place for him to hide.

"Xavier," Grandma sighs, "Apple has been having some dreams at night that she would like some answers to. I thought it might be a good idea to visit Auntie Auber. You know . . . because of . . . Auber's *ability*."

"Dose ponies sure need — " Grandpa starts to say, but is cut off.

"Old man, you're going. Get cracking, my love."

Grandpa sighs with his eyes to the ceiling, shakes his head, and begins to laugh, "Well, I guess I had better pack my tool belt. Old

Auber will put me to work in no time."

Grandma offers no sympathy, "Eh bien, well, she's family and has no husband anymore to help her around the house." Looking at me she adds, "That's what we do. We look out for our elders and take care of them. And, sometimes," she says, looking at Grandpa, "sometimes, we have to make our people remember to honor their elders, whether they're sixteen or sixty." She and Grandpa share a smile.

After Grandpa leaves I turn and ask, "So why exactly are we going to see her? Is it something about my dreams?" Then glancing around for eavesdroppers, I add, "She's not into voodoo, is she? I mean, not that there's anything wrong with that . . ."

"Apple! Now you listen to me, my girl. We Turtle Mountain Indians Do. Not. Practice. Voodoo. Or any such nonsense. There is only one person we worship—the Creator—and don't you go thinking otherwise."

Her eyes soften as she sees my embarrassment, "See, you come from a long line of Metis, or mixed-blood Indians. We're a blend of Cree, French, and even some Chippewa. The missionaries who first came here were French priests—Catholic. Whatever religion first got to a reservation was the main religion that was taught. Many times, this tradition has carried on throughout history."

She continued, "Long ago, when fur trapping and trading was a matter of survival for our tribe, some of our people interacted and intermarried with the French-Canadian fur traders and trappers. French, the language of the voyageurs, became just another tongue for us here. There is no one way to be a Michif. Remember, we usually call ourselves Michif, OK? Some up here follow more of the traditional Chippewa, or Ojibwe, traditions. Some, like our family, follow the mixed culture—including the French influences, both language and food."

She adds a smile with a wink and whispers, "But remember, no one can resist a Turtle Mountain girl! True back then and true today."

"So, I'm still confused. What does Auntie Auber do, then?"

"Well, she has a gift of interpreting dreams. Sometimes dreams are nothing but a release of our daily stresses, but other times . . . well, there is much meaning, which I have a feeling is your case, my girl."

"OK, so how do I go about asking her what my dreams mean?" I ask.

Grandma smiles, "Well, when you ask a favor of an elder, especially one of the traditional Indians who lives up in the hills, you should bring a gift."

I must have had a that-sounds-like-voodoo-to-me look on my face so she explained further.

"Like I said, my girl, we believe in one Creator, and do not worship the created. Some things are traditional up here though. Auntie Auber is a traditional Indian and follows more of the Indian Way. For someone traditional, giving tobacco is what you do when asking a favor from them. It's the life and way she's chosen to live. So, I'll just stop at the store and get some— "

"No, Grandma," I interrupt. "Let me get it. It's the least I could do. You have done so much for me already. I think I can handle buying some tobacco."

"Well, just to be sure, I'll call ahead to give my OK. You can go to Dan's Truck Stop—just down the road. They know me there, and if it's for an offering, they'll let you buy it. I think you need to be eighteen years old to buy tobacco nowadays."

"Sounds good. Hey, Grandma, do they have spicy cheese puffs?" Suddenly, I feel independent and a bit daring. Garbage cans, beware.

So, I'm off to Dan's Truck Stop, which is just a two-minute walk down the road. As I pass the neighbors' homes, I realize how different they are from the houses back in Minneapolis.

Back there, around Lake Minnetonka, there are only imposing structures of beige brick or tower fortresses made of faux river stones. Every house attempts to appear different, but all end up looking the same — built from the same cookie cutter home kit.

Yet here, in the Turtle Mountains, I have yet to see anything close to the color of beige. There's the pink house, or is it salmon? Next to it is a beautiful bright turquoise house that you can't help but smile at. I see creativity and, it may sound silly, but a freedom to paint your house here the way you see fit — not to simply obey the beige rule of boredom.

As I reach to pull open the door to Dan's store, an arm appears from nowhere to prop open the door for me.

"Well, lookie here. It's my favorite little fruit."

My head jerks to the sound of the voice, and before even looking I already know its owner. That man, my mother's old neighbor Karl, was smirking down at me. Alongside Karl looked to be three miniature replicas standing next to him. I'm assuming they're his offspring. From what I know of him already, I think God should have broken the mold after that one. I'm trapped in the little entryway. And trapped somewhere between Heaven and Hell with Karl as the gate keeper.

"Now what brings the Indian princess away from her protectors? Didn't you know there are wild savages in these here parts?"

Karl's minions laugh at this. I look nervously around, hoping to recognize someone, anyone who could help me. But Karl's hapless little entourage blocks the exit door. I'm forced in between all of them. There's something stirring down in the depths of my soul, and I could feel it rising.

"Boys, this here is Apple. Her mama 'n me were real close back in high school."

At the sound of my name the tallest boy spits out the soda he was swallowing. "Apple? Are you kiddin' me?" He glances from me to his dad and back again.

Exactly what is it these guys have against my name?

The tall mini-Karl continues, "Apple. From the looks of ya," he snarls looking me up and down, "that name fits just right."

This comment sends his little brothers into a laughing fit that reminds me of a pack of hyenas circling their prey.

Karl must notice the blank look on my face, "Hey, rich girl. You really don't know what we're talking about, do ya?" He flicks his cigarette on the floor of the store.

"I really think that even in North Dakota littering is a misdemeanor, Karl," I so wisely state. My voice is clearly wavering, and like a carnivore stalking its prey, he can sense my fear. Looking up at him I ask, "And are you the one leaving things at my grandpar — "

After a quick peek over his shoulder, he cuts me off and gets down into my face and whispers so his boys can't hear, "Look here, girl. Ain't nothin' I want more than to send you on your merry way. But first things first. Your mama owes me somethin'. And since she ain't here no longer, it looks like I'll have to collect it from you. Or just give me the money and I'll call it even."

I can smell cigarette on his breath along with disgust in his mouth for me. I try to dig in my purse for any money I have to throw at him, but, oh no . . .

Here it comes. Spiraling up from my heart comes the one thing I do not need right now. Please . . . please not now. Not with him. It's another one of my weird questions, and it's intended for Karl.

Try as I may to quell my words they defy me and push up past my throat and out, "How many greatest hits albums does Barry Manilow have out?"

As I ask this inane question, I can just see out of the corner of my eye that this sends Karl back a step. He's looking at me with widened eyes and mouth slightly open. It's just enough distraction for me to push past him and enter the store.

I run past the entryway and enter Dan's Truck Stop and Convenience Store as quickly as I can go considering my legs are wobbling like lime Jell-O (the only decent flavor, by the way). There are a few people lingering about in the store and I know they saw what was going on in the entryway with Karl and his mini-minions. It seems that in this town some people are afraid to step in when it comes to Karl.

After walking around the perimeter of the store (who knew you could buy pickle-flavored chewing gum?), my heart slows to a nearly human beat and my memory finally comes back to me: I'm here on a mission. A mission to buy some tobacco for an offering to Auntie Auber.

I peruse most of the aisles until I hit the pay dirt in aisle four: personal hygiene products and tobacco. But there's only one problem now. How do I know which tobacco product to get?

My heart skips a beat as I look out the window and spot Karl and his boys gassing up his truck and the oldest tall boy heading in to pay. I quickly grab the nearest package of tobacco from the shelf and head to the counter to pay. I throw down a $20 bill and tell the clerk to keep the change. She looks at the change I left and then at me like I'm Mother Theresa and yells a hearty thanks to me as I run out the side door.

Out the door, on the opposite side of the building from the gas pumps, I peer around the trash bins to see if Karl is still there. I can see his silver truck pull out and head back into town. Even though the coast is clear, my head isn't. I can feel my heart beating fast again like I just ran a marathon, but I need to get back to the house. The entire way home I keep saying to myself, "There's no place like home. There's no place like home." I figure if it worked for Dorothy from *The Wizard of Oz* it'd work for me. After all, it brought her home after a crazy adventure, and I feel like I'm smack dab in the middle of my own voyage. But if a witchy woman peddles past me with a dog in a basket, I'll freak. More than I already am.

Luckily, I'm able to make it back to Grandma's without any more run-ins from Captain Karl and the crew. What in the world does that man have against me and my name? And why does my name seem to send him and his boys into a fit of incredulous laughter? Hopefully, Grandma and Grandpa can fill me in a bit on Karl on our way to Auntie Auber's house. And why would my mother take anything from him? He said she owes him something.

After heading into the trailer (it's really more of a soft shade of cherry blossom), I finish getting ready for our visit to Auntie Auber's. And this time I don't even think of what to wear. I look in my closet, and even with all of the designer outfits I brought, I honestly can say that I have nothing to wear. I mean really. You know what happened to my expensive pumps after my last foray into the bush. And I'm starting to realize that the more expensive something is, the less practical it is.

So, I settle on an old pair of Levi's from my mom's dresser, white button-down shirt, and my (now) favorite cowboy boots. Fashionistas, eat your heart out.

Junior ends up coming with us after he shows up bringing Grandpa a horse halter that needs repair. Apparently, my grandfather is a jack-of-all-trades and can fix anything. I hope he can repair the fear in my heart. Just as we're about to head out down the driveway in Grandpa's truck to Auntie Auber's, we see a cloud of dust kicking up a storm down the street and what looks like someone riding a battled old bike.

Grandma, with a bent smile, puts her hand on Grandpa's arm to slow him down and to wait for the cyclone to approach.

"Wait! Mooshum! Kookum! Apple! Wait!"

I know who it is before the dust settles. Little Inez, or Nezzie, as people up here call her. In the back seat of the Ford pickup Junior is puckering his lips at me, then continues the lip point to the seat next to me.

"OK, OK, I get it Junior! You don't have to yell at me. I'm moving over." Cripes!

Still stewing about the run-in with Karl as Nezzie walks toward the truck, I lean over and whisper to Junior, "Um . . . Junior? What is an apple? I mean, what does it have to do with Indian people? Apple as in Granny Smith? Golden Delicious? Is he saying I'm a frumpy green Indian?"

Junior spits out his soda he was drinking and laughs. But he cuts it short.

He raises one eyebrow and, glancing at my grandparents in the front seat, quickly answers while shaking his head, "I hate dat term. It's a sayin' dat means an Indian person ain't all Indian trough and trough. It means dey look Indian on de outside, but aren't Native all the way trough. Like red on da outside, but white on da inside. Where'd ya hear dat?"

I just shake my head. There isn't time to ask him more, but I get the picture. Karl is trying to take the one positive thing in my life right now—being a part of my Indian Turtle Mountain relatives—and turn it ugly.

How dare someone tell me what I am on the inside? I know that this is my first time to the rez, but, come on! Who is Karl to tell me what it means to be Indian? If I wanted to use a food reference to describe Karl, it would be a prune. Dark and craggy on the outside, disgusting on the inside, with a nasty after-effect to your bowels later.

My mind is brought back to the present as I hear Nezzie yelling again. I move over to make room for her in the back seat of the pickup.

Chapter 13

THE WAY TO AUNTIE Auber's is speckled with dirt roads mixed with rusted mailboxes peeking out from under a hedge of trees and brush. As we drive, my hand taps nervously on the door handle. What exactly is this aunt going to tell me about my dreams? That I miss my long dead mother? Hello! This is not news. I wonder if she ever worked for those late night 1-800 numbers like Sister Star who can foretell your future (for just $3.99 a minute).

I'm shaken out of my thoughts as I glimpse out the window. Oh. My. Gosh.

"Stop the car!" I scream, not realizing that I may have just given my grandparents a heart attack. "Stop, stop right here, please! Pull over!"

Junior cranks his head and responds, "What in da sam hill is wrong with you?"

"Did we hit something?" questions Grandma.

"No," I say. "I . . . I think I just saw . . . yes! Yes! I knew it!"

I bolt from the truck as soon as Grandpa pulls over. I can't believe what I'm seeing. In history class we learned about them, but never in a million years did I think I'd see one with my own eyes.

My hands outspread, I start reeling off facts: "These were mostly destroyed when the settlers moved in, see, and most are worn down from the elements. Anthropologists aren't sure if all were sacred places, or just artistic expressions."

Grandpa, Grandma, Junior, and Nezzie are tumbling out of the truck after me. They seem to be passing looks of wonder between themselves, but I could be mistaken. There's a fine line between admiration and "should we commit her?"

"Apple, what are you talking about?" Junior asks, bewildered.

I'm running down the ditch and back up, stopping just short of the small hill. And there it is.

Like Vanna White, I let my hand gesture behind and wave over the vista behind me as I whisper, "In history class we learned about these mounds. Indian burial mounds. Some of them were effigy, or animal-shaped mounds. Wow."

Grandpa and Grandma exchange looks as they peer over my shoulder to see it.

"And, look!" I yell turning to my right, "There's another one! And four more down there! Just think of all the historical treasures buried in there . . ."

"Oh, I'll tell ya what's buried in dem mounds, Apple," Junior chuckles.

I stop contemplating what I'll name this archeological dig site when the press gets wind of my find and turn behind me. "What? What! You knew about these Indian burial mounds and you never told anyone? But this is important for Indian people!"

Junior nods adding, "Oh, yes, da mounds are really important for people out here, Indians and whites."

I stand waiting to be enlightened but everyone, even Nezzie, can't talk anymore. Their shoulders are shaking! Oh, they're crying.

This is huge. I never thought about archeology as a profession, but sure! I can see it now (although I really don't care for the color khaki, which seems to be a wardrobe staple).

Through tears Mooshum says, "My girl, dose aren't quite Indian burial mounds. Dey're . . . dey're uh . . . septic mounds."

My blank stare meets all four pairs of eyes.

"For the septic system," Grandma adds.

"What . . . what do you mean?" I stammer.

Junior whispers to Nezzie, "Apple lives in da big city, remember, so she don't really . . ."

"What? Are you saying these aren't burial mounds? What's a septic system?" I ask.

"Well," Grandpa states, "it's where country houses send da waste water . . ."

My eyes must give away my ignorance because Little Nezzie pipes up.

"Apple," she says tugging on my sleeve and whispering in my ear, "it's da crapper keeper."

I look around at everyone as they wait for my reaction, their eyes flickering between themselves as they try to predict if I'll be embarrassed. I can't figure out how I feel. Then I look down as I feel a little hand slip into mine. Nezzie's hand is a perfect fit. We all stop for a minute to see flocks of birds of various types fly overhead, some singing and some crowing. I'm finding that the sounds of the city are fading from my memory lately and are being replaced by the calls of birds from early morning to late at night.

Nezzie must be chilly because she puts her other hand into my sweatshirt pocket. It's an odd little hug, from an odd little girl, but

I can't remember the last time I felt like I fit in, and not the odd man out. From somewhere in my belly comes a great wave of laughter that throws my head back. It also sends a sweet calm settling on my nerves.

"Well," Grandma says stifling a laugh, "Auntie is waiting."

As we all head back to the truck (if you look closely you'll see my tail between my legs), Junior pats me on the head. "Yep, we'll make an Indian outta you yet, city girl," he says, and adds a wink for good measure.

While looking back at the mounds, I slowly realize that I keep looking for some "Indian thing" outside of me—like these mounds—and maybe, just maybe, I need to start looking within.

Although, I'll never flush the toilet the same again. Who knew?

Heading out back on the main highway we pass by the Welcome to Turtle Mountain Chippewa Indian Reservation sign again, and once more, even after Junior says he personally painted over that fluorescent green paint, there's the graffiti again. This time it says: "Whites better dead = more for the Reds."

Grandpa, Grandma, and Junior just shake their heads.

Nezzie, not to be left out adds, "Mooshum, I wish they wouldn't do dat. It's ugly. Init?"

Grandma turns and pats her head, "Yes, my girl, it is. Yes, it is."

"I wish it were pretty again. Dat's not nice if people make things ugly on purpose."

I pat her little hand again to let her know I agree.

We arrive at Auntie Auber's house a few minutes later. I'm starting to get used to the mélange of color Turtle Mountain residents paint their houses. There are simply no boring beige bungalows here.

My grandparents chose the lovely (it really is, you know) shade of salmon for their abode. And Auntie Auber chose a tantalizing shade of turquoise for her home. It's the exact shade of the Cortez Sea, which I know because we all went down there when my dad spoke at a medical conference in Cabo San Lucas, Mexico. Let me tell you, my brother had a nasty experience with drinking the local water. Let's just say he and Montezuma got to be real close that trip.

As we're pulling into the driveway, I notice Nezzie is snuggled up next to me in the truck and is twisting my fingers into hers. As I playfully squeeze her hand, it hits me — for years I've tried everything at school to get someone to like me, to accept me, to be my friend. My BFF. And here is my little cousin offering it all to me (and I didn't even have to do my foreign exchange student act!).

Junior gets out of the truck first, and I have the odd sensation of being the one left on the teeter-totter. He strolls up to the porch and bends over to give a kiss to the old woman rocking in a battered old wicker lawn chair.

"Oh! Let me take a look at who you brought, Junior," she giggles.

As I walk up the path, I give her a little (read: pathetic) wave. "Hi. I'm Apple, and I guess I'm your great-niece or . . ."

"Psh! Don't matter what you are, I'm just glad ya came." Auntie Auber's voice rides up and down gently, just like so many people speak up here.

Grandma adds, "Now Auntie, remember I just called you about our granddaughter, Apple, and her little *issue*?"

Shielding her eyes from the sun, Auntie speaks up a little louder. "Well, Xavier don't just stand dere!" she calls after seeing Grandpa. "Can't ya see my railing is off-kilter? I just might slip and fall one a dese days."

Grandpa dips his head to hide his laughter and sighs, "Auntie, I just knew I should bring my tools. I'll have it fixed in no time."

I think Grandma and Auntie Auber share a wink, but I can't be sure.

"Well now, hurry up all of you. I just made some gallette, and now dat I tink of it, I should have made a double batch, init?" she says, patting Junior's stomach.

At least I figured out that gallette (rhymes with mullet, that '80s hair style that some just won't let die) is something to eat. Boy, the food around here sure isn't dainty: bullets and now gallette. But it is good. For the first time in my life my pants are a bit too tight, but maybe it's not such a bad thing to be "filling out," as Grandma puts it.

Walking into Auntie's petite little house reminds me of the aroma of our local bowling alley. It's a mixture of Lemon Pledge and foot odor, but somehow it works.

Holding out a pan, our hostess says, "Hot from da oven!"

Whatever gallette is, it smells incredible. Peering into the pan as I take a piece, I can see that it's some type of biscuit baked in a pan. I take one, but really want two.

"Eh, bien!" (she says it Uhh baaa, just like Grandma) Auntie says incredulously, "You're as skinny as a rail, my girl. Take some more. Look at Junior, he's not shy!" Junior stops mid bite as he starts to protest, but then laughs. He really is a good guy. How does the saying go? That's right: he's a gentle giant.

Nezzie had been hiding behind my legs the whole time and finally reaches around to grab some gallette.

"Well, look who's here," Auntie whispers softly looking at Little Nezzie. "Come here, my girl, and say hello!"

Nezzie comes out from behind me and slowly walks to our hostess. She looks back at Grandma and gets an encouraging nod, then keeps going right up to Auntie's apron.

Auntie smiles as she bends down to kiss Nezzie's head. But instead she stops and takes a great whiff of the child's head. You heard me. This is one odd crowd we've got here, and it's all trickling down into my gene pool.

Taking another smell of Nezzie's head, Auntie whispers, "Ahhhhh, da smell of youth," and walks back to the couch. Looking wistfully up at the ceiling, she adds, "when da only mustache I had to worry about was a Kool-Aid one."

Nezzie looks at me as she tilts her head, shrugs her shoulders, and runs out back where she spies an old tire swing hanging on an ancient weeping willow tree. I'm watching her, remembering how much time I used to spend outside when I was her age. Outside was my refuge—under the shade trees, of course. No need for sun exposure and the risk of getting too tan. But I'm starting to rethink that—sunscreen. I haven't thought about using it the last few weeks. My tanned skin is starting to look like chocolate milk.

"So, Apple," Auntie starts as she peers at me, "what's dis I hear about you. You've been dreamin', init?"

Looking at Grandma I stammer, "W-w-well, I guess I've been having some dreams." Grandma nods to me, encouraging me to keep going. "And well, I have one that keeps recurring."

Why on earth does she keep calling everyone "Init?" First Junior, and now me.

A look is shared between the two older women. "Go on, tell her. Auntie has a way with understanding dreams."

And so I begin telling her about one of my dreams—the one about a baby bird in a nest that has black threads of hair throughout it. And also, I mention that an Indian was beckoning me.

Auntie sits back in her rocker with eyes closed. "Oh, yes. Dat's a good dream, and pretty easy to interpret. Da person beckoning you is an ancestor inviting you, asking you, to come back home."

Shaking my head in confusion I ask, "So they're asking me to come back here, to Turtle Mountains?"

"No, my girl, dey're asking you to come back to your Indian roots. Dat's what home is if you're a Native person, init," she pauses, looking to Grandma, "It can be up here, but sometimes it's any Indian community."

"OK, I guess that makes sense. Can I ask you about the other part?" *And why you're calling me Init*? I want to ask.

"Eya, yes," she nods.

Auntie is rocking away with no hints of talking or opening her eyes. She has beads clicking between her fingers. So, she must be praying for help to interpret. At least she doesn't bring out voodoo dolls. This continues for an uncomfortable ten minutes.

Finally, she begins, "Da woods is your life. Da nest is your family. 'N dat baby bird is you, my girl. And dat black hair woven in da nest? Why dat's a remnant of your mama still creating a home for you, protecting you even dough she's not on dis earth anymore."

Whoa. I may need another piece of gallette after this. Or two. Or ten.

"Thank you, Auntie! I never knew dreams could mean so much—have so many messages."

Auntie just continues rocking, but now her face wears a grin.

Grandma is the first to break the silence. "Apple, remember what you're supposed to give her?"

Give her? Oh, I guess I forgot to give Auntie a kiss on the cheek. I wonder if they do the double-cheek-Euro kiss here. So I move in to give her a peck, when out of the corner of my eye I see Junior waving his hands and shaking his head. Now I'm not known for being too socially adept, but even I understand that one. So, I fake right and pretend to flick an invisible food particle off Auntie's shoulder.

"No, no, Apple," Grandma whispers to me, "What do you need to give her, *offer* her?"

I must have the deer-in-the-headlights look because Junior, sweet savior, Junior clears his throat to say, "Apple, didn't you buy something to offer Auntie when you went to Dan's Truck Stop?"

Oh my gosh. I totally forgot the tobacco I bought back at the store when I ran into Karl and his mini-minion sons. Who wouldn't want to block that encounter out? Let's see, what did they say this tobacco was for? That's right . . . when someone offers to do something for you in the Indian community one way to thank them is to give them a gift of tobacco. A prayer of thanksgiving.

Digging in my purse, I manage to find the paper bag and contents I bought earlier. As I walk to Auntie and her chair I glance left then right to pick up any clues from either of my relatives. Nothing. They're giving me nada. So, I just let go and proceed with caution.

"Auntie, here is an offering for helping me understand my dreams, and uh, maybe helping me with something else." I'm hoping to ask her if she knows why I get visions and ask such odd questions to certain people.

The closer I get to her, the more Junior and Grandma are leaning in to watch. I hand over the bag and give a little curtsy. I'm not exactly sure where that curtsy came from, but if it's good enough for the Queen, it's good enough for Auntie Auber, by golly!

Looking in the bag, Auntie says with a little smile, "Well, I . . . I . . ." and stares back at me, then into the bag again. "I . . . OK. Tank you, my girl. Come sit down by me." Auntie is smiling, taking it all in as she continues rocking in her chair.

Cool. My first tobacco offering. "Peace, man," I say looking back to Grandma. She just shakes her head. OK, I guess I need to be more reverent, but I have no filter when it comes to my mouth. Why couldn't I have been born here? Then I'd understand how to do traditional Indian things. But I'm learning. Can you be an Indian just because you were born that way? I take a few steps to head for the couch when Junior suddenly grabs the bag from the coffee table where Auntie placed it. He senses something is up by her reaction. He grabs it and runs out the front door and opens Pandora's Box.

Chapter 14

"APPLE!" HE CHUCKLES. "Is dis what you gave her?"

"What?" I say defensively, running to catch up next to him. "Grandma said to buy tobacco, so that's what I did."

Peering again into the bag, Junior is barely able to speak through his laughter "Apple, dis is Nicorette. You know, gum people take to stop smokin'?"

"Oh, I . . . I just grabbed the first thing I saw in the tobacco aisle at Dan's." Then, recalling my encounter with Karl, the words tumble out, "and he and his boys scared me because Karl said I owed him something and to give him money." Big breath. "And then I asked him some weird question . . ."

Soon I was leaning against the truck. I've lost my strength. Everyone is now on the dirt driveway. All turn their eyes to me when they hear Karl's name mentioned.

"My girl, come here," Grandma whispers. "Now don't you go worrying about Karl. He's all talk."

"I knew he would cause some trouble!" Junior shouts, with Auntie quickly patting his shoulder.

Trying to calm him down, she adds, "Let's not get too worked up over Karl."

Sensing something more was going on I ask, "But why would some Indian guy I don't even know be like that? Why did he and his boys stop me at the store?"

Letting out a sigh, Grandma begins, "Well, my girl, Karl's family lived next to us when your mom was younger. Oh, he was crazy about your ma. I guess in love with her. Came from a good family—they'd help anyone in a pinch. Karl, though, he was different. He was always trying to scam people out of their money. He never wanted to work for his money. Your mom just always turned Karl down when he'd ask her out in high school. She would talk to him, sometimes even try to help him out with school work. He would try anything—music, poems, building things for her—hoping that they might help win her."

Now I'm more confused than ever. "But what does any of this have to do with me?" My back is to all of them. I don't want to face them. Partly because I'm sobbing. Mostly because snot is running down my face.

"Don't you know?" they all ask incredulously.

Auntie is the first to answer, "Apple, have you seen pictures of your ma? Maybe da ones in dat hallway at your kookum's house, your grandma's house? Look especially at her high school graduation picture. It's like you're a perfect copy, init?" She looks to everyone.

My head is swimming with images of anti-smoking commercials, my mom, bird nests, and someone named Init. Confusion doesn't even start to explain how I'm feeling.

"I did see that picture, right Grandma? That one with my mom and the redhead?" I ask turning toward her. "But my mother was beautiful. I'm . . . I'm . . . well . . . look at me." All I see when I look down is my tears mingling with the dirt, making a muddy pool.

"It's so hard for a beautiful soul to truly see how others see them. But, my girl, you are beautiful. And the fact that you don't know it, makes it all the more true," Grandma says gently, pulling me into her with a hug.

Junior calms a bit and chimes in, "So you can see why Karl was shocked to see you—you're da spittin' image of her. I guess some guys never get over deir first love. Don't worry about him doin' something to harm you. I'll take care of him. You're just a reminder of what he could never have."

So, this is what it feels like to have family. This is what it feels like to be loved. Even so, Karl is still a creeper.

Before leaving there's still one more thing that's bothering me and I have a feeling that Auntie Auber is just the person to help. It's about my weird habit. You know the one. The one where I have to say some odd thing of which it never makes sense to me. It's funny though, because it really isn't happening up here in the Turtle Mountains at all. Well, I guess there was that one time I asked Karl how many albums Barry Manilow has out. Whenever this mouth diarrhea occurs, the things I say never make sense to me—yet I always see a glimmer of recognition amid the indignation from its recipient.

Auntie is sort of odd. Just outside the realm of normalcy to maybe shed some light on it. Birds of a feather flock together, I guess. Just please tell me if I ever get anything more than a Kool-Aid mustache fifty years from now. Or even next Thursday.

Following her as she walks to back to the house, I ask, "So, there's sort of this other thing I was wondering about. Wondering if maybe you know what's going on with me, when I . . . when I . . ."

Patting me on the back as he tries to maneuver around us, Junior says, "Spit it out dere, Apple. Auntie's show is coming on and if she misses her *Wheel of Fortune* fix she somehow thinks Pat Sajak will die."

"I don't tink, I know sometin' will happen to my Pat. I still can't believe he turned me down and hired dat Vanna girl." Auntie says with a wink.

I open my mouth to ask how she almost replaced Vanna White, but quickly cut that thought short as Grandpa walks up the porch steps and shakes his head letting me know not to go there.

"So," I begin, still in the doorway holding the screen open, "here's the thing. I have this habit. Well, not a habit in the good sense. A habit in a way that I don't understand."

Auntie isn't quite looking at me. She walks back in the house and sits in her chair across the entry focused on the TV and her show.

I continue while holding the screen door open, ". . . sometimes when I meet people I have this image in my head. I never understand what it means, but then I seem to blurt out a question related somehow to that image. It never seems to go over too well."

Auntie doesn't hear me at first. I start to tell her again, but before I can finish she puts her hand up in a stopping gesture. She grabs the remote and clicks the TV off as she rises from her chair.

Finally! I am going to get some answers to my long-awaited questions. This is it. Auntie will tell me what all this means.

I'm wrong. While she crosses the room her face falls. Exhaling loudly, she takes the screen door from my hand and says quietly, "Apple, dis is not the time for more questions. I gave you answers for your dreams. Today's troubles are enough for today. You go home now and visit again, my girl. Pat gets jealous, don't ya know, if I'm gone too long." And with a quick sniff of my hair and pat on my cheek, she quietly closes the door, crosses the room returning to her chair and TV. And to Pat Sajack. *Wheel. Of. Fortune.*

To my utter embarrassment, Junior witnessed the whole thing. My total shutdown from Auntie. But he was kind enough to say nothing, only reached out and gently grabbed my elbow to guide me back to the truck.

I'm not sure what everyone is talking about on the ride home. I don't remember what scenery passed outside my window. I don't notice Little Nezzie cradle my hand in hers. But I'm aware of being there again. Not quite a piece of here nor there, but hovering somewhere in between. In the dreaded middle again.

One thing I need to know is why Auntie keeps calling Junior and me "Init."

With my hands still interlocked with Nezzie's and her sleeping peacefully against my shoulder, I whisper to Junior, "Who's Init?"

"What? What do you mean, Apple?" he asks quietly, so as not wake Nezzie.

"Init. You know — Auntie kept calling us that. Sometimes you say it, too . . . Oh! Is it some kind of word in the Michif language?"

Shaking his head, he rolls his eyes, "Apple, you do know dat she was saying 'isn't it, or ain't it?' Dey just sort of roll it together up here in da Turtle Mountains, and it comes out 'init.'"

"OK, so how was I supposed to know?" I yell a bit too loud and Nezzie stirs.

My little cuddle partner chuckles as she drifts off to sleep saying, "Init? A person? Apple, you're so silly."

Face. Red. Me. Again. Embarrassed. But then this little girl calms my heart as she pats my leg. I lean over and sniff her hair. It's a mixture of crayon and dandelions. Maybe that is the smell of youth?

"Best friend," she pats my arm and says just loud enough for me to hear as she leans against me, drifting off to sleep in the truck seat next to me.

That's all she says. Two words. And they mean the world to me. I've never had a best friend before. I've never had someone who loved me no matter what stupid things I said. I've never had someone who could look past my exterior and into my heart.

But I have one now.

* * *

Later that night as I'm getting ready for bed I empty my pockets. I feel something soft in one of my sweatshirt pockets and pull it out. A feather? Nothing grand or beautiful about it, but a soft downy feather. Maybe from a sparrow? I took my sweatshirt off after the "septic situation," and I had it hung over the back porch railing back at Grandma and Grandpa's house. Someone, anyone, could have had access to it. It's the porch closest to the alley. The alley that Karl drives through each morning. Why would he do this? What does the feather mean? I'm a bird-brain? A cuckoo? Or maybe a warning that if he catches me, he'll tar and feather me? It is a warning, isn't it?

I add it to the growing collection of things—or warnings: a jar of dirt, some sage, a few juneberries I found on the front porch last week, and now a feather. Not sure why someone is giving them to me. And not sure if I should be leery of them, or like them.

Chapter 15

LITTLE NEZZIE AND I are spending a lot of time together. This summer she is attending Four Winds American Indian School, just up in the hills from our house (Notice I don't even call it a trailer anymore? Home is where the heart is.).

June passes and it's getting deeper in to summer. We fall into a routine. Me helping around the house and Nezzie going to school. She comes to our grandparents' house after summer school today and throws her little Hello Kitty backpack on Grandma's couch.

"How was school?" Wow. I can't believe that just came out of my mouth. That is such a "mom" thing to ask, isn't it?

Nezzie looks up at me straight-faced and replies, "School. It's taking up too much of my time."

Can't argue there. From the back room a deep voice says, "You gotta go to school and you gotta eat!" Except when he says "eat" it came out "yeeeet." I guess Grandpa means you have to feed your mind, as well as your body.

The only thing Nezzie likes about school is her teacher, Miss Berta. I've met Berta a few times around town and I have to say, she is the skinniest person I've ever seen. Her face is all angles, but it's her stomach that I can't help but stare at; it's concave, as in caved in on itself. Yet she's always snacking on something, but where the food goes, nobody knows. Berta's hair is barely an inch long, spiked in all directions, but somehow it works for her. I think I remember seeing her at my grandparents' house during my welcome party that first day I arrived up here. She was going to town on the venison, gnawing on it like her tongue was stuck in a metal trap.

Nezzie talks on and on about Berta and says that when she grows up she wants to be a teacher, too. At least she has something to look forward to at school. I despise school, with Marcia and her little snotty comments and how people smirk every time I mess up. The only thing I like at my school is the three o'clock dismissal bell. That's right, pack your bags; we're going on a guilt trip.

We've started taking walks after Nezzie comes home from summer school. On our walk last week, she shared a story. Nezzie said she and her big sister were talking to one of the new teachers' aides, a young white woman from Iowa.

When she first met Little Nezzie the teacher said, "Oh, you're from the local tribe here? So, how much Indian are you? I mean, what percentage Indian are you, Nezzie?"

Well, apparently this didn't go over well with Tara, the big sister. Tara told me later that this question of asking Indian people "how much Indian are you?" is a horribly impolite question to ask. Actually, Tara said asking Indians this question is really racist and assumes that people have the right to know everything about Native people. I didn't understand (what's new?), so Tara said that blood quantum, or a percentage of Indian blood, is what people are really asking for. So someone might say, "I'm half" or "I'm one-fourth Ojibwe." Yet, this very way of cutting Indian people up was based on outsiders trying to "determine" who was Indian for reasons like land ownership. You should read up on blood quantum. It just might make your own blood boil.

So, after the teacher asked, "How much Indian are you?" Nezzie looked down at her body, shook her left foot, shook her right foot, wiggled both arms, looked up and said, "Well, all of me!"

Her big sister let this new teacher know that she was asking Nezzie a loaded question when Tara replied, "We're not saying anything about percentage, teacher, but do you know what percentage of idiot you are?"

* * *

Back to our walks. A lot of times Nezzie points out who lives in what house. Morinville isn't that big, so after a few times I've already got the lay of the land. There's always one house we have to walk past. Nezzie insists. It's Jeff and Junior's house, a dilapidated wood house across from the Dollar Store. The Dollar Store: who knew you could buy a shirt or duct tape for only a dollar . . . a dollar!

Jeff is Junior's roommate. Berta just happens to be Jeff's sister, so sometimes Nezzie gets to see her there, too. Everyone is connected to everyone else up here. It reminds me of a spider web, people attached everywhere by a silvery network. Anyway, Jeff lost his job last year at the car repair shop and hasn't found another one yet, so he spends most of his time underneath the hood of his Chevy two-ton truck. Guys — I'll never understand their fascination of cars. What's with them? Put gas in them and they run. But Jeff must have polished and tightened every square inch of that truck.

This time we arrive at their house just after lunch and knock, but we have to jump off the stairs as the door flings open. Junior stands bare-chested in the doorway eating a corn dog. Actually, he's double-fisting it, a corn dog in each hand. He smiles when he sees us, wipes the ketchup off his lips, and then licks it off his finger.

"Can't waste my daily vegetable servin.'"

Running up the three stairs, Nezzie flings open her arms as she makes to hug him. But Junior's balloon belly beats her to it. Her little head bounces off his gigantic stomach, her head whiplashes back, and she flies down the stairs.

Junior and I reach her at the same moment. Her tiny lips are quivering as she tries to hold back the tears. We each grab one hand and gently pull her up.

"Oh, Nezzie," I quickly say, trying to get her mind off the hurt. "Look, you've grown!" And I hold out my hand level to show her where her head meets Junior's belly. He winks at me, catching on to my plan.

All her pain is erased by hearing this. Wide-eyed she whispers, "Really?"

"Assault with a deadly weapon," a deep voice laughs from the doorway. "Roomie, you better put a shirt on, man, or we'll have another casualty on our hands."

"Jeff!" Nezzie yells. "Oh, Jeff, you're here!"

He steps down to where she's standing and pats her head. Jeff is movie star handsome with carved cheekbones, tanned well-toned arms, and soft black eyes.

My little friend squeals, "Jeff, sing for me! Sing me that song."

But he walks past her. "Oh, Nezzie, not now, I've got to figure out where this transmission fluid is leaking from. Next time." And he walks to the hunk of junk parked in the driveway and slides under it with his tools.

Nezzie is in love with Jeff's voice. Apparently, he's a gifted singer, but Nezzie can never convince him to sing for her. He sings at powwows up here in the Turtle Mountains with a drum group called Four Directions during the annual Turtle Mountain Powwow, but I haven't heard him sing either. I wish he would wheel out from under the Chevy and just sing for the girl. But no. Adults are stuck in their own worlds and sometimes they pass by moments they can never get back.

We must go past Jeff's house once a week on our walks, and he always has some excuse, "Sorry, Nezzie, my throat hurts," or "I just have to return this phone call." You know the drill.

Yet it never gets her down. Jeff is a nice guy, just too busy for us kids. Nezzie tells me what her favorite songs are each time we begin our walks. She acts like today will be the day he'll sing for us. Each day she's always sure that this day she'll finally get her wish. One day I hope she will.

"Come here, my girl. We'll make some snacks for everyone." Berta, like a skinny fairy godmother, appears in the doorway and says, while looking at Junior, "We don't want anyone to starve to death." Berta is just as quick to make sure Nezzie doesn't cry after her brother gave us all the brush off. But Berta's staring at Junior a bit too long. Hmmm, interesting.

* * *

It's now already the first week of July, and so the preparations begin for the upcoming annual Turtle Mountain Powwow. The next afternoon we're back at Junior's house where Berta is helping with the dance clothes. Jeff, of course, is elbow deep in oil under the Chevy out front. The entire living room is a mess of fabrics and two sewing machines. I only read about powwows at school during our annual week-long unit on "multiculturism." How nice, my school spends a whole five days talking about people who had some pigment in their skin. And then we spend the rest of the time on dead white men.

One year I asked my sixth-grade teacher why anyone with dark skin is called a "minority." That word seems like it's a bad thing. I told him, "What happens in a few years when the white population is going to be the smallest group and the Indian, Latino, African American, and Asian people are the majority? Maybe call the whites a whiteority, or a minor-blanco?" He didn't know what to say. You can't argue with facts, folks. And it's a common fact that the best food comes from these "multicultural" groups anyways. Tacos? Yum. Haggis—which is oatmeal stuffed in sheep stomach from the Scottish people? No thanks. Let me put it in easier terms: maple syrup (discovered and perfected by Native people) good, escargot (snails eaten by French people) bad. Case closed. Those with mucho pigment win.

So anyway, I had no idea how much planning it took for a powwow. I sort of thought we would just show up. Not even close. I also didn't even know that Nezzie and Junior danced. It's not something that ever came up. Nezzie outgrew what she wore last year, so she needs something bigger to wear.

"So what costume are you going to wear now, Nezzie?"

And with my question, the room halted to dead silence. Good heavens. What did I do now? My motto should be: open mouth, insert (size 10) foot.

"Apple, costumes are for Halloween; outfits are for Indian powwow dancers," Berta explains gently.

Junior adds, ever so humbly with a wink, "And if you're on loan from da great Ojibwe nation, like myself, den you call it regalia." Berta laughs loudly and catches me looking at her. She blushes a little and goes back to her sewing. Interesting.

Auntie Auber comes over that afternoon, too, and is working on sewing tiny beads onto both Junior's and Nezzie's outfits. I can't believe that it takes her over on hour just to finish sewing beads onto one square inch! I grab a small handful of the beads and can barely see the center hole—and my great-aunt is sewing these so tightly together that the soft cotton material is hidden behind them. Wow.

As Auntie sews she explains what design she's making. It's a floral pattern, unique to the Ojibwe tribes, who historically lived in the woods and always admired and were connected to woodland flowers. Actually, Ojibwe still live in and love the woods and flowers! Each flower Auntie is sewing is a bright color ranging from red, to turquoise, to yellow and is connected by a vining trail of thin green beads with leaves attached throughout. Picasso, eat your heart out. You ain't got nothing on this Native art.

"So, Auntie, why does Nezzie have flowers on hers, but you're sewing some ribbons and a beaded humming bird onto Junior's?"

"Well, see, just like every dancer is diff'rent, we have to make every outfit diff'rent, too." Patting Nezzie on the head she continues, "Our girl here loves to be outside, so I'm honoring dat part of her heart." And tapping Junior's back she adds, "And Junior goes to each person in life and finds the good in dem, bringing out da best. Humming birds do da same ting to flowers. His beading reminds him to keep doing dat."

"Man, dis shrunk again dis year!" Junior stands in front of the mirror in the living room putting his clothing on, trying to fit a feather bustle around his lower back, wiggling his ample behind.

"Eh bien! It's your stomach dat grew, my boy!" Auntie laughs. "Give it to me, I'll let it out. Again."

Junior just winks at me and gives his belly a rub. He melodramatically shakes his mile-long, midnight-black locks and turns to Auntie, "Don't hate me because I'm beautiful." What a ham. You are what you eat, I guess.

"Come here, Apple," Berta nods to me, "you can help with Nezzie's shawl — she's going to be a Fancy Shawl dancer this year. That's what her mama danced." I look up when she says this and my face must have shown my dislike when I hear her speak so matter-of-factly about Nezzie's mom. The mom that's nowhere to be found and who abandoned this sweet little girl.

Berta holds up the small black shawl with beading and fringe dangling around the edges. "Now, Nezzie, you go get me some more yellow ribbon. We need to fix the ones that fell off. Oh, was your mama ever a beautiful dancer. She won a prize at every powwow she danced!" she tickles Nezzie under her chin.

After she left the room I shot off, "But how can you say anything nice about her mom? The mom that abandoned her?"

"Well, sometimes a person has to hear about da good tings, because we know too many bad tings in life. Her mama had such a way in her dancing dat made you believe she would just up and fly away. She'd hold onto her shawl with both hands and make jumps and moves for every drum beat. Not everyone can do dat." Auntie explains.

“So, this used to be her shawl you’re working on, but you made it smaller? The one that Nezzie will wear?”

“Eya, yes. Sometimes a person just loses dere way. I tink her mom will find her path home again, Apple. It’s a bit big for such a tiny girl, but Nezzie knows that da fringes should never touch da ground when she’s dancing.”

Auntie nods to me and whispers more, “Every girl wants a hug from dere mama, init? Dis shawl is our way of giving dat to Nezzie.”

“All right, I guess.” For some reason nobody will let me hold a grudge up here. Against anyone. Humph.

While we work mostly on the shawl, they also let me help with Junior’s beaded vest (size XXXL). Junior: size triple X, triple threat. Apparently now I am the thread cutter. Oh, what an honor. But I have to admit, it’s cool to be a part of something. It’s been a long time since that’s happened. Err, wait. Really never.

Chapter 16

THE NEXT FEW WEEKS pass by and I spend more time with Grandma and Grandpa helping them around the house. Grandpa lets me work next to him in his garden out back. Back home I never wanted to get my hands dirty doing yard work, but here it is different. Here the cool earth between my fingers seems to take away all time. I'm out picking beans and potatoes for three hours and never even notice the time fly! Except for all the biting flies. Nature is not for the weak.

Grandpa is amazing. I mean really. Here's a World War II veteran who came back to his reservation, was the first Indian in the state to ever finish college, and was an all-state basketball champion whose team (seriously) played the Harlem Globetrotters and won. On top of that he's been a tribal council representative for Morinville, but only after he was tribal chairman. Whew! And I thought my collection of participation awards took the cake.

But here's the thing: Grandpa would never, and I mean not even once, brag about his accomplishments. In fact, everyone up here will brush away any compliment or praise with a sweep of their hands. What a difference from back home.

It's funny. Up here the Indian people have so much beauty in their lives, but not the superficial kind. Not fancy homes, designer clothes, expensive cars, or even prize-winning roses like back home. But what they do have is a quiet, gentle knowledge of the beauty that's found in life through four main things: family, faith, nature, and humor. You can't buy that. Not even at the Dollar Store. Eya!

In a way, I feel as if I'm starting to shed my old self. Two months ago, you would never have seen me wear the same outfit twice in a month. Now I pretty much wear the two pair of Levi's from my mom's closet and her old cowboy boots. And I've never felt better about myself. Who knew? Indian family and reservations: the best kept beauty secret. Or maybe it's me understanding who I am.

Back to the beans. So, I'm next to Grandpa in the garden; both of us kneeling as we pick. As I start eating some green beans he stops and stares at me. I don't see him at first, so I keep throwing each one in the air and try to catch it. I'm pretty good, if I do say so. As I notice the look on his face I stop quickly.

"Oh, I'm sorry, Mooshum; I shouldn't eat these yet, should I?"

Laughing he answers, "No, my girl, you eat as much as your little stomach can take. It's just dat . . . it's just da thing your mama used to do. She'd toss up her popcorn, nuts, grapes, anything really—and catch it all in her mouth. Da more I watch you, Apple, da more I see your mama in you." And with that he moves to the next row to tackle some overgrown tomatoes, grinning all the way.

My heart is smiling. Maybe my mother never really left me. Maybe she's with me, in me, even today. After all, one grape-catcher can only beget another.

Grandpa stops and stares at me. "Apple, see dis?" He holds up a packet of daisy seeds.

"Well, um . . . yes. I can see it."

Taking a seed into his hand, he says, "Now, some may tink it's just shriveled up and lifeless. But da seed, it knows better. It has to die when I plant it in the ground."

OK, so what's up with this agriculture lesson?

He digs a small hole and lays the seed in it, then gently covers it up. "Now, dat seed changes and begins a new existence." Grandpa lip-points to a row of yellow and orange flowers next to me. "It flowers into a whole new life. But just because you can't see it way down in da dirt, doesn't mean it isn't dere, isn't alive."

Huh, well, I'm not sure what this was about, but, maybe he thinks I'll go into farming. I really don't do bib overalls well. Does anyone?

I finally ask something, or actually admit why I hate cemeteries.

"So, well," I hesitate, "I'm sort of afraid of dying. You know, after my mom . . . If I stay away from cemeteries, then I guess death will stay out of my life."

Mooshum whispers in my ear while hugging me, "Oh, my girl, here's a secret: You're gonna die!"

So much for gentle words of wisdom.

He continues, "Apple, da day you are born you've begun on da path to die. But, it's da journey on dis path, life, where you need to focus. Don't be afraid of death — it's just another form of life. One we can't see. But just because you can't see something, doesn't make it something to be afraid of."

He's so smart. And so right, I guess. Still . . .

* * *

And so the days melted into more days, laughter and love spilling over my time spent with my grandparents, Junior, all my relatives, and of course Little Nezzie, who has snuck into my heart. After all, we're best friends. It's taking me forever to remember the rest of my relatives' names, but they all seem to know mine. Even after all these summer weeks, I'm still learning their names—apparently, they don't believe in naming kids Tom, Dick, or Harry. Spot or Jane aren't on the top ten lists for names either. Here, let me explain: I have a Cousin Bricks, an Aunt Chip Chee, an Uncle Dunseith, and another cousin (twice removed—I have no idea what that means) named Gypsy.

About that last cousin, I tried to use one of those mnemonic memory tricks to remember his name. Remember those tricks? You try to think of something that rhymes with their name. However, my cousin Gypsy didn't take it so well when I called him Tipsy. So, I pulled out another memory trick where a person imagines an animal on the person's face which triggers the actual name. Now I call him Moth. Not sure if it's helping me any that I carry a fly swatter around looking for rogue insects. Gypsy gives me a wide berth when I walk past him.

* * *

Auntie Auber comes for coffee a few times since my last visit to her house. Whenever she shows up at Grandma's house, she gives me a little wink and a nod. Sort of like we have a little secret between us. I guess we sort of do. If no one else is around she whispers, "My girl, any more dreams?"

"Just the same one, Auntie. Just the same one."

Looking around, like she's on a covert operation, she always answers, "Well, dat dream is telling you a message. Until you learn and take it to heart, it will keep coming to you."

It sort of reminds me of Nezzie's comment about school. Sometimes things seem like such a waste of time, whether it's dreams or education. But I guess if you actually take it to heart and learn something, you can move on to the next lesson you're meant to hear.

I feel that up here in the Turtle Mountains, my thinking is clearer. Maybe getting away from the bustling city calms me. Grandma says that when we have too many things on our mind, like money, anger, or trying to be popular, our thoughts get side-tracked and we block out connections. And connections are what's really important. Also, I don't seem to have any of my weird visions or impulses to pose weird questions to anyone up here. There was only that one to Karl. What was it? Something about "how many albums does Barry Manilow have out?"

Now I'm starting to notice how much I see Karl and his boys around town. Most mornings he cuts through the block in the alley out back heading to work. That's a little too close for comfort. And a little too close to my bedroom window. It would only take him a few seconds to throw something in or to try to steal something, since he's so bent on getting paid for whatever my mom had of his. Every so often I catch him staring at me from his silver truck, glaring at me. His boys aren't any better. They stare when I'm at the post office. On the sidewalk with Nezzie. At the McDonald's. Sometimes his older boy is in the back of the truck and yells, "Hey, it's da white Injun!" It makes the hairs on my neck quiver. Are they following me? Or . . . are they stalking me?

* * *

One positive thing I'm catching onto up here is how much Native people revere their elders. Obviously, Karl and his boys haven't learned this one yet. Most others, though, show respect. The kids make sure the elders have what they need, especially when it comes to food. We kids always refill their coffee cups. We clear the table and start the dishes while the adults visit around the table. And we do this without even an eye roll or a sarcastic comment! It's not automatic, and from what I can see some kids need reminding, but it's expected.

It was sort of different for me back in the city. At home my stepmom, Judy, jumps at the sight of an empty juice glass. She waits on us kids. But in the Turtle Mountains, the younger ones wait on the elders. Without being told. What a concept. Yet it feels good to take care of someone else for a change.

It's not just refilling coffee, either. If an uncle or auntie walks into a room and all the chairs are full, it's up to the young ones to get up and offer their chair. I learned that quickly. And guess how? Yep, I blew it.

So, the second week up here I was comfortably sitting in Grandpa's cushy recliner watching the Cubs game. It's Cubs games up here, only the Cubbies games allowed in Grandma's house. Mooshum walked in the living room to a full house. Everyone was at the house to watch the game between the Cubs and the Minnesota Twins, and there wasn't an empty chair anywhere. So, I always like to sit in Grandpa's comfy recliner right in front of the TV, and when he walked in he paused, looked around and smiled at everyone. But he just stood there. Pretty soon all eyes were on me. So were the pointy lips. First it was Grandma, then Junior, and then even Nezzie lip-pointing at me and then up.

I actually didn't make a scene (Grandpa was waiting for me to get up but wouldn't think of embarrassing me). After finally getting up and moving to the floor next to his chair, I felt a little pat on the head from him as he nestled in to cheer his team on.

"Why that ump is blind!" Grandma commented after her favorite player struck out. "Get some glasses, ya old coot!"

"Yeah, I guess I could get you your boots," Mooshum replied, as Grandma looked at him and just shook her head. A second later, I peeked back at him and he just winked ever so quickly at me. He is sooo playing up this "hearing loss." I think it may be what I love about him best—his sense of humor. To him, life is just too short to get mad or crabby. Grandpa has worked hard his entire life, but along the way he had fun and didn't take himself too seriously and doesn't stress out. Life happens, whether we like it or not. Having anxiety or anger isn't something my Indian relatives dwell on. They have an attitude that things will work out if you put effort into the good things in life.

I think my blood pressure has gone down quite a bit trying to live this way.

Chapter 17

IT'S FINALLY THE DAY of the annual Turtle Mountain Powwow and Junior is over early getting his vest let out (again). He is a Traditional dancer and his costume, I mean outfit, regalia, is incredible: around his lower back is a feather bustle that his uncle gave him, the beaded vest that Auntie worked on is worn over a black shirt with tiny shells attached around the cuffs, in his hair he's wearing a clip of horse hair, and it's all complete with his grandfather's moccasins—beaded in the traditional Ojibwe floral design.

Junior lets me know that Traditional dancers' regalia is always kept close to nature. And fittingly, he carries a turtle shell. It reminds him of where he comes from. He says each dancer chooses designs and items that are meaningful to them.

We drive in a big caravan out to the powwow grounds just outside of town. It's basically a wide-open field, next to a wide creek, and has a circular wooden awning on the outer edge with bleachers on the inside edge. The middle area is where the dancers and drum groups will be once the powwow starts.

Little Nezzie is a riot of color in her outfit. She's a Fancy Shawl dancer and has beaded moccasins on with leggings up to her calf. Her favorite color is pink (isn't it all little girls'?) and so Grandma and Auntie added rows of every imaginable shade of pink, magenta, and rose around her shawl and leggings. The fringe on the shawl, which was repaired, is a mixture of both yellow and white ribbons. This morning I braided her hair into two braids, which fell on either side of her perfect little face.

Me? What am I wearing? Why, since you ask I'm wearing my (now) favorite pair of Levi's, Mom's cowboy boots, and at the last minute I grabbed the only clean shirt I had: my turquoise Dior t-shirt. Judy picked it up last fall for me in New York.

Junior looks me up and down, focusing on my t-shirt. "You're a CC."

"Hmmm? What's that?" I ask.

Laughing, he says, "Country Club Indian." But he adds his famous wink.

"Yep," I add right back at him, "and don't you forget it." Funny. A month ago I would have been humiliated, thinking he was being cruel. Up here, I'm understanding that teasing is a way to show love between Native people. Sometimes, it's a way to gently guide someone back to a good place. You tease someone instead of yelling for them to be better. Grandma said Native humor has many aspects, but one thing it is used for is to bring a person who is out of line softly back into the community. So, I saw an older cousin tell his daughter (when the girl was wearing jeans ripped right in the backside), "Oh, so you're going for the Kevin Costner look now? A little *Dancing with Wolves* behind the scenes view?" Apparently, this movie is the butt of many jokes in Indian Country (ha, get it?) 'cause the two main characters are white and one shows his rear. And the movie was supposed to be about Indian people, not white people playing Indian. Anyway, the girl laughed at her dad's comment, and then went and changed her pants. Native humor isn't mean; it is just a way to gently tease someone back to community.

Now I'm realizing that there just isn't one way to be Indian, just like there isn't one way to be a Minnesotan, or even one way to be an American. You've got to put your own spin on yourself, just like the powwow dancers individualize their regalia. Just like the Michif language is its own spin on the French and Ojibwe languages. I'm part doctor's daughter and part Indian daughter, and I guess my style shows it. I am the melting pot. Just not fondue. I'm not fond of fondue. Baer's scab fell off into the fondue pot last Christmas and it caused a minor meltdown from me. I couldn't figure out why the marshmallows I dipped in the chocolate fondue were crunchy. Again, another vomit story. Sorry.

The powwow MC, master of ceremony, announces that it's time to begin, and all the dancers take their place in line. The Grand Entry is incredible. As Grandma, Grandpa, and I take our seats, the eagle staff enters the grounds carried by the tribal chairman. Following him are the veterans carrying the flags.

"There's Junior!" I feel as excited as a kid who just saw Santa.

He looks up as he dances with everyone else; all are moving in a clockwise circle. Of course, Junior looks up and winks. The rest of the Traditional dancers are jerking their heads and bending to resemble animal movements: stalking prey, searching for shelter, or flying. Junior is sort of doing that, but his moves look like a turtle opening the fridge, checking for leftovers. Still, I feel my heart swell watching him, my cousin (was it third cousin, or fourth? Who cares!).

"Where's Nezzie, Mooshum?"

Smootchie lips point the way. She doesn't even look up here at us. Nezzie's attention is consumed as she holds out her bright kaleidoscope-colored shawl, one hand grasping the end, and spreads her arms out. First, she moves in a tiny circle to the left, spinning around, then in time with the drum moves just as fast to the right. All the while taking a step to each drum beat, allowing her fringe and ribbons to flit this way and that. How can such a tiny thing put all those steps together and create one smooth dance that makes her look like she could take flight at any second?

Can my smile get any bigger? I lay my head on Grandpa's chest, as he sits next to me. My head is dizzy with what I'm taking in. This is my first powwow; my first chance of being a part of my Indian family. And I notice something . . . nobody is staring at me, pointing me out. It's almost as if . . . almost as if everyone thinks I belong here and fit it. The colors, the drum, and whirling dancers must be getting to me, so I continue to rest against Grandpa's chest. Maybe I didn't eat enough this morning because I feel weird, a little woozy. I can hear bits of Grandma and Grandpa's conversation, "jingle dancers . . . healing dress . . . Grass Dancers swaying . . ."

Grandpa's heartbeat is getting louder and louder as I lean on him; it's thumping in my ears. Bum bum . . . bum bum . . . bum. But then the heartbeat speeds up and rises in my head. I bolt up and look at him. Is he having a heart attack? Oh, Mooshum!

Wait, why can I still hear the beat echoing in my chest, but I'm not leaning on him anymore? Glancing at him, I don't see Grandpa in any trouble. Everyone is still watching the dancers.

Oh. My. GOSH! Am *I* having a heart attack? A fainting spell, maybe? My core feels as if it will explode from my chest. Bum bum . . . bum bum . . . Then the beats crescendo faster and faster. I look at the dancers, but my eyes are drawn to the drummers, just outside the dancers' circle. The drum, deer hide stretched over a wooden frame, bellows each time it's struck. What is going on? The drum beat mimics my heart beat, or is it my heart echoing the drum? I'm confused. I don't feel normal.

My breathing is smooth and deep, yet bottomless. Everything starts to move in slow motion. As I exhale I see the tops of the trees being pushed back, obeying my breath, their leaves whispering inaudible words. When I inhale, I see the dancers' fringe sway towards me. In and out, leaves moving this way; the beads and shawls circle, keeping time to my breath.

Why can't anyone see what is happening? Hazy eyesight is keeping me from looking at my relatives sitting next to me. WHOSH! WHOSH! WHOSH! My senses are being assaulted. Rushing through my veins, my blood surges in unison with the rippling waters of the creek behind me. I can actually feel the blood flowing through me, but also mingling with the movement of the creek's current, the little stream just behind me. My heartbeat, breath, and blood are in harmony with my surroundings, pulsating peacefully with the earth.

It seems like time is hanging in limbo. It's as if I'm alone and nobody is here. Am I dying? A gentle arm wraps around me.

"My girl? My girl?"

"W-w-what?"

"Apple, are you OK?"

I emerge, as if I've been away in a coma, shaky. "Grandpa, I . . . I . . ."

His kind eyes look right into my soul. It's as if he's reading me. Nodding his head, he asks, "Did you feel something?"

"Yes, I . . . it was like . . . like I understood it. No, that's not right. Like I was every sight and every sound here at the powwow."

He gently took my arm, and then put his hands on my face. "Yes, yes, I understand, my girl. When you shed a tough outer covering, you discover harmony inside. Sometimes dere is sacredness attached to a place. Each place affects people differently. It looks like you know dat now, hmm?"

And the thing is, I know he understands. He pulls me to his chest to hear his heartbeat again. It calms me. My breathing returns to normal. As I try to fathom what just happened to me, I catch Grandma and Grandpa's conversation, "when you attend a powwow, you are a part of it, not just a spectator."

I think I get it. Wow! Sound the music, throw the confetti, and bring out the cake! I am no longer a spectator here, I BELONG! I am a *part* of it all. My body melts with the sights and sounds of my Native relatives, land, and culture. For once I am included in what is around me, not bouncing between two worlds, not stuck in the middle. I start to feel humbled, like I don't deserve what just happened to me.

"Eya, yes, it sure is a good ting to come to a powwow. Init?" Grandpa winks at me.

Whispering, I lean over, "Yep, it sure is." Talk about putting the pow in powwow! "Do you want anything to drink? I think I need some water, and maybe some air."

"Yes, you go ahead, Apple." Then Grandma looks at me with her head tilted sideways, "You sure you're OK, my girl?"

"I think I just may be better than I've ever been."

Chapter 18

MY LEGS ARE A little wobbly as I make my way down the bleachers and across the parking lot to the concessions. In the background I hear the MC saying, "and we'll be back after a fifteen-minute break to have our competition round for the Little Miss division!" I need water. My throat feels like I've gargled with sand. Communing with nature is tiring stuff. Whew! Bumping into people, I make my way around to the food wagons. I probably look like a drunken sailor coming off a three-week bender. Avast, ye mateys! The crowd parts and I head to quench my thirst.

Walking past the concession stands, I wave to Berta, who is working at the burger stand. Her spiked hair looks like porcupine quills on steroids. Leaning on the counter, I order a bottle of water from her.

"So, what do ya think of your first powwow, Apple?"

"Well, it's just about the coolest thing I've ever seen. Wait, I mean it's the coolest thing I've ever been a part of." She nods in agreement, gnawing on a big pickle.

Looking around, Berta asks, "So, who all came with you?"

My head is still in the clouds, so I don't hear her the first time.

Clearing her throat, she repeats, "So, um, who's with you here?"

"Oh, the usual: Grandpa, Grandma, Nezzie, and . . ."

"Junior?" She asks, with one eyebrow hovering on her peaked forehead.

I'm still not all with it in the brain department, but I answer not really looking at her, "Yeah, he's somewhere around here."

Berta's mouth is open (with juicy pickle parts on her tongue), as if she's just about to say something more, but I continue. "Hey, what's that thing I heard the MC say? Something about the competition? A Little Miss competition?"

"Oh, yeah, that's the dance contest, but for little kids. Starts at two o'clock."

I grab my bottle of water from her, "OK, thanks! I'll bet that's the one Nezzie's in. I want to be sure to get back in time." Glancing at my watch, I figure I have ten more minutes. Thanking her again for the water, I walk around a bit, gulping it greedily.

Ahh, sweet aqua. I pour a little over my head to drench my sweat. There's a shady area I see by the parking lot, so I walk over to seek some shelter from the heat. I still can't believe what just happened to me back at the powwow. Did it really happen? Yes, I giggle to myself, it really did! And once I start to chuckle it comes out in great torrents of laughter raining straight from my heart. I lose my balance and lean back on a car to steady myself. My eyes closed and head upturned, I just continue smiling and laughing.

Instead of a cool breeze fanning my face, now there's a waft of stench, the same one that filled my childhood. Alcohol. Whiskey. Judy's influence helped my dad get some help with his addiction. But where's that smell coming from now?

"Well, looks like we got ourselves a rotten apple, here, boys," a gravelly voice says from right behind me.

I know that voice and it yanks me back from my thoughts. Quickly my eyes open, my head swings around only to find that the truck I'm leaning on is silver. The same one I've seen following me around town. Karl's truck. And it seems that I'm only two feet from him.

"Sounds like she's goin' crazy laughin' like that. What do ya think, fellas? With her rich daddy she might need to buy some therapy."

As I spin completely around, I come face to face with Karl. He's sitting in the bed of his truck with three or four men. His two oldest boys are sitting in the truck cab. There's a paper bag wrapped around a bottle they're passing around. And Karl's got a grin as big as the Cheshire Cat.

"Ha! Dat girl comes from a long line a' crackpots," the guy to Karl's left says as he elbows another man.

"K-Karl, I . . . I'm just g-getting some air," I spit out while trying to slowly back up. But I back up right into a tree trunk. There's nowhere to go.

Karl has a knife in his hand and he's carving something, "Why, you're out here pretty far from everyun', girl." His eyes search over his shoulder and then set back on me. "Tsk, tsk, tsk. You ain't scared, are ya?" Continuing to wield his knife, he slices the thing in his hand and eats it straight off the blade.

It takes every bit of courage, but I have to do something. I need to know. "Have you . . . have you been leaving things f-for me? G-giving me things back at my grandparents' house?" In my head it sounds like I'm yelling, but I know it's just above a whisper.

He spits out what he's eating. "Ha ha ha! Just what am I leavin' you? Huh?"

Karl takes a swig of whiskey. The other men continue passing around the bottle, but one guy touches his arm and shakes his head. "Leave her be. She ain't her ma."

Karl shoves him hard enough so the man stumbles out of the truck bed.

"I tell ya what I'm givin' ya now, *Apple*. A warning: I'm warning you again. And here it is: I want what yer mama owes me."

He squints in the sunlight, but he's staring right at my neck. "That fancy necklace o' yours might just be worth somethin'."

I cover the gold flower-shaped necklace with my hand like it's actually keeping me from falling over; like it's what's keeping me alive. My dad gave me this last Christmas. He never really said what the design means. I have no idea what it's worth, but I know I'll never give it away. Especially to Karl.

The sunlight bounces off Karl's black hair. His cheeks are the ruddy red of a drinker. It's then that I notice what he's been slicing and eating. It's an apple. And there's a glimmer of recognition in his dusky eyes that frightens me. Wait! That's symbolism, right? Him eating an apple. Or is that a synonym? Oh, why didn't I pay better attention in English class? Let me think . . . synonym means the same. Or is it cinnamon for the insane?

Bubbling down in my throat I feel a familiar sensation. I can feel a question; an odd question rising and it's just at the tip of my tongue, "K-Karl . . . when's the last time you were at— "

From out of nowhere the sun is blocked out. A massive midsection stands between me and the silver truck. For a minute, I think it's Karl blocking out the world. But it's a giant.

"What da heck, man? You know dere's no liquor on da powwow grounds." Junior's enormous arm rips the bottle from Karl's hand

and throws it behind the trees. I peek from behind Junior's back and notice the rest of the men have run off, leaving only one man there. My nightmare.

"Oh, Junior, yeah, man. I, uh, knew that. Some of the boys, you know, brung it. And— " Karl jumps down from his truck and grabs his cowboy hat that fell to the ground.

Junior doesn't even wait for him to finish talking. "The Red Road, Karl. Follow the Red Road." And that's all he says. He gently takes hold of my elbow and leads me from evil. I turn around, knowing I shouldn't, and Karl is staring at me. His lips twist into a half-smile and it makes my fear whole. His two sons spit on the ground and follow Karl back to the truck.

After we're a good fifty feet away Junior only says, "Come on. Nezzie's competition starts in a few."

I yank my arm from him. "Junior! Didn't you see what was going on back there? Karl, he, well, he almost . . ."

Stopping mid-stride, he turns to me. "Yeah, I saw it. I saw it. Karl's just don't got enough sense to just leave it alone. But he's all talk. Don't worry about him."

Tears start to slip down my face. I reach for Junior, to lean on his shoulder, but instead end up getting blocked by his gut. My body is bent over at my waist and my head is resting on his stomach, which feels like a mushy counter top.

"Oh, now," Junior pats my head. "Apple, don't worry. You're all right."

I lift my head up and stare. He wipes my tears. Then tilts his head and holds out his sausage-sized finger saying, "Pull my finger." And his face breaks out in a huge grin.

"Junior, how can you joke at a time . . ." I can't even finish because my shoulders start to shake. I'm laughing. I'm laughing at this great beast in front of me. How does he thaw my fright so fast?

We both walk back to watch Nezzie. As we cut through the concession stands Berta yells out, "Hey, Junior, Apple! Hi!" She's waving wildly. "Ya want a burger? I can make ya a double!"

Waving her off, he replies, "No, tanks."

Oh Junior. How can you be so fearless, but so completely clueless?

I tug at his sleeve, "Uh, you do know that's she's totally crushing on you, don't you?"

He looks at me like I'm speaking Russian. *Nyet*. Looking between me and then back at Berta, Junior's eyebrows start to furrow. I can see a giant question mark above his head. "Berta? Me? How do you know dat?"

"A girl knows, trust me."

He looks down at himself, his belly, then shakes his head; his dark hair falling from side to side. "But, I'm . . . well, you know."

"Oh, Junior," I softly say. "You are one of the most beautiful souls I've ever met. That's what caught Berta's eye. The rest is just a bonus."

There's a softness that comes over his eyes. We hear the MC announce "the Little Misses should come to the dance circle." He takes one quick look glance back at Berta and smiles to himself. Before we reach the bleachers, I turn back and ask him, "Junior, what was that thing you said back there to Karl? Follow the Yellow Brick Road."

He spits out the water he's drinking and hoots. "Ha! No, we're not talkin' *The Wizard of Oz* with Dorothy and the Tin Man. I just reminded Karl of the Red Road. It means for Indian people to walk on a right, straight, and sober path in life; a clean body, mind, and spirit." I know alcohol has had a really horrible impact on Native people. I know how kids suffer, because even though my dad is white, alcoholism messed up his ability to feel. I like this Red Road. I'm going to tell my dad about this. But maybe my mom already told him about it? Did you, Mom?

I just shrug my shoulders. Maybe I still don't understand everything, but I know now that's OK. I'll never forget my experience here. Nothing can cloud that, not even Karl.

"Hey, Apple?"

"Yeah, Junior?"

"Watch out for dose flyin' monkeys."

* * *

Nezzie dances her little heart out with the other little girls in the competition. Her fringed shawl takes flight, and she leads our eyes around the dance circle. Taking a step to each drum beat, she is a blur of pink. I have no idea how they would pick the prize for the most skilled dancers. Of course, I know who I would pick. Jeff is down singing in a drum group. You can't hear his voice independently, but Nezzie smiles at him. At least she gets to see him sing. The competition ends, and the MC calls for the little kids to go back and sit with their families and wait for the winner to be announced. We all hug her as she reaches us. Her little fingers are kneading my knuckles. She's nervous waiting for the results. We all are.

"And, it was tough, folks, to decide," the MC says. "But here we go! Third place goes to . . . little Annie LaRock! Second goes to . . . Kimberly Red Bird! And first place, our new Little Miss Princess goes to . . . Kateri Azure! Oh . . . oh, wait folks; let's not forget our honorable mention . . . Nezzie La Belle!"

Our heads whip around to see Nezzie, to comfort her in her loss. How could she not have won first place? Her face is in her hands. Grandpa pats her leg. Oh, Nezzie. I start to put my arms around her when I see her pull her face up. Tears are streaking down, spilling onto her pink outfit. I would erase all the good that happened to me today if I could just make her stop crying.

"Apple, did you hear? Did you *hear* dat?" she whispers incredulously, her eyes as large as saucers. "I won *honorable mention*!" With that she jumps up on Grandpa with her hands pumping the sky. "*Wow!*" Her smile lights the sun. "It's better to be honorable, instead of just first place, init?" I can hear her echoing Mooshum's way of saying "dat."

Grandpa replies, "Dat's right, Nezzie. It's da best ting you can be."

We stay for the rest of the afternoon, taking breaks to watch the dancers, eat, and visit with everyone. I don't want the day to end, but the crowd started to thin, so we decide to head back home.

Nezzie sits next to me on the ride home and her little head rests against me. She holds her arm out vertical next to mine, "Coco . . . nut."

"Hmmm?"

Pointing to her arm she says again, "Coco." Then pointing to mine she says, "Nut. See? We're da same color. Like da outside of a coconut."

The same. We're the same. Sometimes you feel like a nut, sometimes you don't. And in this case, I'm overjoyed to be nutty. Why was I ever trying to cover this brown skin?

Chapter 19

THERE IS ONE ISSUE still that I don't know how to deal with. And it comes up every Sunday. It's church. It's not that I don't like, or want, to go to church with everyone. That's not it at all. For me, going to church this summer has been the one place where my mind is calm. Everyone is facing forward, which means I can blend into the crowd. And when you've lead my life, that's always a good thing. Also, up here this town is so tiny that the only gym, the only ball field, the only meeting hall and industrial-sized kitchen is up at the church. So, most things in the community happen up here. You've got God, grand-slam homeruns, and goulash all within twenty feet of each other.

Sunday morning up here is a routine. Grandpa gets up at zero-dark thirty and is making pancakes and bacon and jigging all the way. That I like.

We pile into the truck and cruise down the highway with the local KAWL radio station blaring Hank Williams, Jr. and Travis Tritt (remember, we're in country music land up here). That I like.

We file into St. Francis Xavier church, just outside of town and take the second to last pew on the left side. I sit in the middle between Junior and Nezzie. Talk about being between a pebble and a mountain. That I like.

It's after the Mass that I don't like.

"Well, let's go," Nezzie says.

"Eya, yes, let's go," Grandpa says.

"Come on, my girl, you come," Grandma says.

"It'd be good for ya,'" Junior says.

"Umm, no thanks. Not this time," says I.

We're not talking about going to the church hall to have donuts and coffee, folks. My Turtle Mountain clan wants me to go for a walk. After church. Out back. Up the hills. For a visit. To see it. The grave. *Her* grave. In a cemetery. I just haven't been able to do it all summer. Of course, I know I should visit it, but, you know, I have that thing about cemeteries. It's a phobia of death I still have. I run from it. Maybe if I visited her grave I would have to face the fact that she was really here, was really my mother—not just a figment of my imagination. I guess maybe it's not graves really, but having to meet my mother for the first time when she's six feet under.

Junior told me that up here there isn't a cemetery crew like in big cities, so the relatives tend to the graves. They cut the grass, pick the weeds, plant flowers, and pat the tombstone as they say a quick prayer. So once a month after church most of the congregation spends a half an hour or so taking care of their relatives' gravesites. Everyone but me, that is.

It's not that I don't love my mom. Of course I do. It's just that I've never met her, and I don't want the first time to be where she's six feet underneath me. What do I say anyways? *Sorry, Mom, for killing you. I appreciate you dying so I could live.*

And if I went up there I'd have to walk on dead people. That alone gives me the willies. Plus, the freaky fact is that in a cemetery everywhere I step I imagine walking and sinking into the ground, mingling with rotted remains. You put one foot in (someone's putrefied mouth), you put one foot out (of goopy brains), and you shake it all about (their decomposed ear). I've never been a fan of the Hokey Pokey. Death sort of freaks me out.

Grandma gives me a little peck on my cheek and tells me they'll be gone just a few minutes. She nods to a couple of women in the little church kitchen making the weekly luncheon and tells me when she and everyone are done at the cemetery we'll eat. It looks like a pretty good spread, too.

"We'll be just up the path through the woods. The cemetery is off to the right. Your mama's grave is right next to the oak tree — the tallest one," she says as she peers up the path showing me with her eyes where it is.

I should follow them. I know I should. And that embarrasses me. Everyone up here has done nothing but welcome me. Shown me what family means. It isn't just my mom's grave they cleaned up; it's all of the ancestors'.

This summer I've heard about them all — all of my ancestors. There was Great-Grandma Elizabeth, whose house burned down when she was a newlywed and unfortunately lost all she had. Then there was Uncle Fabian who won the Congressional Medal of Honor for pushing five men out of the bunker when he saw an incoming grenade and threw his body on it saving not only those men, but managed, in his last few moments of breath to send coordinates for an air strike during the Vietnam War.

Of course, I couldn't forget Great Uncle Joseph who, during WWII, was stationed in Papua New Guinea and befriended a clan of pygmies (really!). These Natives in the jungles only wanted to survive and continue living their lives like they had for centuries, but found themselves submerged in the Pacific theater of a world war. A world war that these pygmies had little to no knowledge even existed. Mooshum showed me an old faded black and white photo of his brother, Joseph, standing in front of a hut, towering over a native pygmy chief. I always get so confuse about whether a person is a "great" uncle, or just an uncle up here. But it doesn't matter, says Grandpa, just show the proper respect and call them Uncle. Who cares if it's a great or not. I asked Mooshum once why—how two people so different—my Uncle Joseph and this pygmy man, got to be such good friends amid the ravages of war around them.

Grandpa just tilted his head and winked, saying, "We natives have to stick together. Anyone who loves da land, da One who created it, is family. We're all brothers and need to stick together—especially during war." He should have told that to the Nazis. Brotherly love, they did not have.

I love hearing about the relatives' stories and where they were buried up back in the cemetery. And about the mark they made on the world. I'm amazed at how heroic they all were. I'm not just talking about the soldiers. That's a given. But I'm humbled by the stories of my ancestors, both men and women, who bore the brunt of Indian Boarding Schools, of those who simply tried to make ends meet, of those who fought the fight of racism as they applied again and again for jobs at stores that still had signs on their windows which read, "No dogs or Indians."

Indian people are the best storytellers I know. And this is coming from someone who loves her TV. And her *National Enquirer*.

And her *CSI*. Nope, Native people win hands down. Junior says the reason for that is because years ago, during the winter months, Indians would pass the cold days by telling stories. The stories would be passed down from generation to generation. It was a way to teach the next generation about their history, but also to teach life lessons. And it makes sense, because when you hear stories from the past, it connects you to your future. A connection is what I'm after. When Grandpa tells stories, he uses his hands with wild gestures and turns his voice into a great bird which we all follow to see where it lands. I wish it were winter so I could hear some traditional storytelling, but I know now to respect the culture. At least I'm trying my hardest to respect it and learn it.

Chapter 20

I'M LURED OUT OF my thoughts as I wait for everyone to return, when out of the corner of my eye something in the little church catches my attention. It's the stained-glass window to my right. The sun glares through it almost blinding me. Shaking my head to clear my mind, I laugh a little realizing how deep in thought I was. No wonder those monks didn't talk much. It's easy to get lost inside your head in a church, but it's like someone is holding a magnifying glass up to the sun through those windows and it's hitting my eyes just so. Time to bail.

There's a little garden just outside the back door. I've seen it through the window and I figure it's a safe enough distance from . . . from it. The cemetery. Bouncing down the stairs I take in the deep scent of the Turtle Mountains. I tell ya, if I could bottle that smell, I'd put Calvin Klein to shame. Or Axe cologne. Boy, I'd really like to put Axe out of business. That stuff reeks.

Nezzie was the one who actually showed me what I was smelling in the air up here. It's a mixture of wild sage, sweet clover, and those pink wild roses strewn about. There's a tiny garden in the back of the church. It's laid out in the shape of a medicine wheel: a circle divided with a cross in the middle of it. Each quartered section has a native plant: sage, clover, and wild roses. But I'm not sure of what this fourth section has in it. It's in the back part of the garden and towers above everything else. Red berries dot the tall plant, almost like a tree. If it smells as vibrant as it looks, my nose will be in for a treat. This little country garden is where I spend time after church when everyone else is up the hill in the cemetery.

I get closer to take a look and sniff. And sniff. And sniff again. Mr. Markman, my white-board-loving math teacher, had nothing on me. I was going to town trying for the life of me to figure out what this last unknown half-tree, half-bush species was.

"Chokecherry."

"What?" I gasp spinning around.

"Chokecherry. That's what tree yer smellin'. Tree don't smell that good."

I know that voice and it's the last one I want to hear now, "Karl . . . I . . ." I look frantically around for help, but to no avail.

Karl's black hair looks almost blue with the sun bouncing off it. He's wearing a blaze-orange vest over a black t-shirt and camouflaged pants. He has his tall, oldest son, Rafe, with him. Karl also has a gun.

Looking closer at the boy next to him, I glance down and notice that Rafe is holding a can of neon green spray paint. Green spray paint. We hold eye contact for a few minutes with a look of acknowledgment flitting back and forth between us. I know where I've seen that paint before, and he knows it, too.

"Dad, I'll meet you back at the truck. I need my scope. This one ain't good for nothin'. I gotta ditch this paint now." And with that,

Karl hands Rafe the gun and takes off down the road, but not before mocking me saying, "Rich girl."

Nodding to me after Karl leaves, Rafe leans in closer, "I was going grouse huntin' with my dad but this seems more interstin' here. Have you come up with the money you owe my pops? Huh, rich girl?"

His sneer sends a chill up my spine and a warning call down to my soul.

Family! Hear me!

My eyes are frantically looking left and right; where did Grandma say they were? Up the path . . . through the woods . . . to Grandmother's house we go?

No! No! No! Apple, for once in your life think! What was the way Grandma said to find them? What path was I supposed to follow?

"You're not scared, are ya? Just give me what your ma owes my family and we'll call it even." He seems to be slowly moving towards me.

"I . . . you . . . what are you doing here, Rafe?"

"I tol' you, girl. I 'n my pops, were huntin' back in the woods. But he's not here anymore. Shame." Bending down within inches of my face he points to my gold necklace again and continues, "That could just about cover your debt. Hand it over." I sob as I start to hand him the necklace.

Looking behind him again he says, "What are you doing here, Apple? Why aren't you up with your family? What's the matter, girl? Scared of a little cemetery, Apple? HA!" He throws his head back and laughs while he says my name like it was tart in his mouth.

"I, well, I . . . we went to church and we decided to . . ."

Looking around, then back at me, Rafe slowly realizes, "Oh, I see. You're all alone, my girl. Rich girl. White Indian."

"Listen Rafe," I say as I steadily back up toward the church's clapboard siding, trying to put as much distance between us as I could, "I don't know what you have against me . . . and my mom for that matter . . . but I don't owe you anything. Whatever you think my mom has of your dad's, I promise, it's not in her room anymore — "

"WHAT DO YOU KNOW ABOUT ANYTHING?!"

Rafe's rage is palpable. His pupils have constricted as hard as his heart. Now I can see the resemblance with Karl.

"You don't know a thing 'bout me or my dad. You don't know nothin' 'bout your ma either!" His arms, flailing, emphasize his frenzy.

"Well, R-R-Rafe, I'm here in the T-Turtle Mountains t-trying to make sense of everything especially my mom — "

He rips the garden plot to shreds with arms thrashing back and forth. I've heard that if you can get a violent person to look you in the eye sometimes they stop what they're doing and focus on the fact that you are a human being, too (who knew my CSI shows would come in this handy?). But when I look at Rafe's eyes all I can see staring back are murky pools of frenzy. If eyes are the window to the soul, his eyes would have inspired Dante to keep on writing about the circles of Hell.

Trying to calm him I stammer, "This isn't supposed to be like this. Here," I whisper, still clutching my necklace. "If this is what you think you're supposed to have to make things even — "

"YOU ain't got NO idea about how things were *supposed* to be." Rafe's mouth is twisted as he speaks.

Backing up against the church's back wall, I'm digging my feet in as if I might climb up and away. The wood siding is carving into my shoulders and my eyes keep searching for safety.

"YOU have no idea what was supposed to happen. What shoulda happened! Your ma and my dad—your ma and Dad . . . THAT'S what was supposed to happen!"

"I don't know anything about what went on between your dad and—"

"Well, it's high time you did, Apple. Did your mama name you that?"

His gaze sweeps behind him, looking for witnesses. It's almost as if everyone can sense this ominous teen and scatters before him. I can hear the clanking of the dishes from the ladies back in the kitchen, but my voice is paralyzed. So this is what a caged animal feels like. This is what prey feels like.

"Well, my girl, Apple is a fitting name for the likes of you," he spits. "You're one of them white Indians. Apple—white on the inside and red on the outside. Your ma would never have wanted that, my girl."

Rafe continues shaking his finger right in front of my nose whispering "my girl" over and over again. His hot breath is fanning my fear.

"W-why do you keep saying that?" I cry, trying to hand him the necklace. "I-I don't know you're s-so obsessed with my mom, but why are you doing this? Why?"

Roaring with the force of hated, "Because your ma and my dad were supposed to be! Not with no le blanc! Not some white guy! Those whites are trying to water down our Indian blood. Your ma was a traitor to her own race. My own ma could never live up to the memory of your mom. Made us kids' lives hell. Pops never even gave my ma a chance. Still doesn't. All he talks about is getting back what your ma has of his. You and your ma are traitors! Don't want no traitor owning nothin' of my pops!"

And then it happens. Again. My visions. Coming out once more at the most inopportune time. In my mind I can barely make out a misty image of Rafe's dad, Karl, a much younger version, leaning over an old stereo, humming along with the music. Karl's face in the vision is calm and peaceful—almost happy. It drastically contrasts with his son before me. From the pit of my soul arise words, formed within my depths and rushing past my panic and out. Out to confront Karl and his kid.

"When's the last time your dad was at the Copa? The Copacabana?" I level off, having no idea what it means.

But apparently, he does.

Chapter 21

MY WORDS CAUSE RAFE to stumble back while blinking nonstop. It's just enough of a distraction for me to see my escape. I reach out quickly and grab my necklace back.

Then I spring into action pushing past him while he is slightly off balance. And slightly out of his mind. Looking out past the churchyard, I know where I'm headed. And I need to get there fast.

Dodging around him I jump over what's left of the garden plot. Ahead of me is the dark woods and behind me is dark hatred. Only one choice—upwards and onwards. The entry to the woods is just across the grassy area, surrounded by a thicket of bushes and tall grasses.

Please, please, family—HEAR me! I yell internally. It's as if my worst nightmare is coming true. The one where I have no voice and cannot, hard as I try, cannot scream. But this is real.

I can hear Rafe cussing behind me. He's close enough that I can make out his boots scraping through the garden and across the backyard of the church as he follows me.

"You shoulda never have done that!" he roars. He wears his anger like a cloak.

Turning behind me is no use. I know it will only slow me down. I have to use my instincts to gauge how far away he is, and how to find safety. All of my mental energy keeps running through the directions my grandma gave me.

But there's at least seven paths leading in different directions, Grandma! Which one, which one will lead me to . . . you?

The incline through the forest is getting steeper the higher I run, with tree branches whipping my face with each step I take. Like a drum, my heartbeat pounds in my chest. The pulsing blood rushes like a locomotive in my ears. It's so loud it's blocking out the footsteps behind me. But this time is so different from what I felt at the powwow. Now I feel my body mingling with and battling darkness. Rafe has a gun. Would the ladies making lunch in the church hear the commotion? Can my family hear this?

"Ahh!" A scream escapes from me as I feel a hand grab my ankle. Turning behind me on the steep path, I see Rafe's face contort with rage. He begins pulling me towards him. My leg burns with pain as he twists my ankle trying to get a better hold. Sweat beads on his forehead as he yanks me over rough branches. I can feel a warm trickle of blood seep down my leg.

"Now SHUT UP and get back here! Give me back that necklace! I'll give it to my dad so maybe he can just leave it be!" he bellows.

The ground is still wet from this morning's rain, and his left foot slips. It skids just enough for me to kick free, grab a sapling, and veer to the left under a rotted tree that had fallen.

"Just like your ma! Running away from Indians!"

His words frighten me, but I can tell by the echoing sound I'm getting farther away from him. Up ahead I can see a clearing on a hilltop. Is that where the cemetery is? Is that where the graveyard is? Where my family is?

After three or four minutes I glance behind me to look for Rafe. To my amazement the path is clear in back of me. The path in front of me is clear. I stop and lean against a tree trying to catch my breath, my body doubling over.

I've felt alone before, but this is altogether something else. To be pursued by a force who—

Run! My body overtakes my brain as it spots someone running back up the path towards me. The only place to go is up to the clearing, and that's exactly where I head.

Reaching the top, I don't stop to look over my shoulder this time. I can't take that chance. To my right is the cemetery on the open crest of the hill, but I can't see anyone there.

There. Is. No one. There.

How can this be? You said you'd be up here at the cemetery! Where are you when I need you the most?

I decide my only chance is to run up and across to the other side of the hilltop graveyard, and to head back down. If I can double back and swing down and around this hill, I'll end up back at the little church. Back by people. Back by family. Away from Rafe.

It's only about twenty-five yards across the clearing to get back down in the cover of trees. I can do this! Like a track star setting her foot in the block, I hear *Go!* in my head and jump into action. At the end of the clearing, there's a small construction machine, a backhoe, which is in my way,.so I have to veer to its right.

"I knew you'd come runnin' back this way." An arm grabs me. I run right into Rafe. He was hiding behind the backhoe. I must have gotten turned around back in the woods. That's the only way he could have gotten ahead of me.

"Oww! Rafe, let go! You're hurting me. I never did anything to hurt you or your family!"

Holding my wrist, he whispers, "Yeah, well, as they say, my girl, like mother like daughter."

I must have had a puzzled look on my fear-filled face.

"Oh, you're just like your ma. I can tell you are. She hurt my pops. She hurts us still!"

"But, what are you talking about? What did she do to you that makes you hate me so much?"

For a second, the question softens him, then regaining himself he answers, "My dad loved her. Told me one time he woulda done anythin' for her! But she never loved him. Said she could never love anyone who didn't want to better the world. Told him he was greedy. She always said: you have to better the world. Not just live in it."

I see my chance to talk some sense into him. But he still has a firm hand on my wrist. And now I can see his other arm has a firm hand on his gun.

"So, she didn't love your dad. You all can be . . . happy still. I've seen you driving around town with your mom and dad. At least that's something. Let the past be." Of course, it's a lie. I mean I did see them drive around town together, but his mom never had a smile on her face, just a look of solemn acceptance.

For a moment time stops as he holds his head down and sighs. The deep breaths of a person whose soul is wounded.

And then I feel the grip on my hand tighten.

"'Sides," he says with darkness shadowing his face, "I said your ma owes us for what Dad gave her. And since she ain't here, you need to pay up. Give me that fancy gold necklace now!"

An alarm goes off in my head, and again, I know what prey feels like in the hunt.

With that he brushes up against the large backhoe while stepping closer to me. The gun he still has with him clanks against the machine's door. But as he lets go of my hand to push the door out of his way, I jab him in the elbow and fly around him again, leaping into space.

That's the last thing I remember. No, make that the last thing I remember Rafe saying. I tumble into darkness. A total blackness devoid of any of the five senses. Except one — my sense of sound. I hear it. And then I hear it again.

BANG!

BANG!

Chapter 22

TIME IS FUNNY WHEN you're unconscious. A minute can seem like a day, and a lifetime like a second. All around me I sense silence and the coolness of being in a cocoon.

Blackness and silence is all my mind feels. And then. And then I dream my dreams. Again.

I am in the middle of a sparse forest splashed with poplars and birch trees. In the distance I can make out a splashing sound, I try but can't make out who is making the noise, until a few feet in front of me I see three young people swimming in a shallow pond.

One of the Indian youth in the water is beckoning me. She walks out of the water away from her two companions, who I instantly understand are my ancestors who are with her in the afterlife. Then she turns to me and walks alongside me, staying to my left.

Smiling, the most beautiful sounds come out as she says, "My girl! My girl. Apple, love. How long I've waited for you. As the woman walks toward me I know from the recesses of my soul that it's my mother. As lovely as life. Her long, raven hair blows behind her. She's walking toward me, staying on my left, always my left, with outstretched arms. And as the wind blows through her hair it catches on a branch beside her. A few strands of her hair get tangled in a branch. And on the branch is the nest caught between a tangle of trailing branches. It's set just above me and I can see a tiny baby robin with its indigo blue egg cracked and set aside.

I look closer at the nest. Intermixed with twigs and grasses are threads of black hair. My mother's hair creating a nest, a home for me. Not of brick and stone, but of heart and soul.

My mom is in front of me, to my left, now standing by the nest. She reaches up and grabs hold of the loose strands of hair and weaves them intricately around the nest. The last thing she does is gently, ever so gently, cradle the baby bird in her palm, lifting it out and placing a kiss on its cheek. At the same time, I feel her soft lips on my own left cheek.

"Courage, daughter. I will always be with you, Apple. I have always been with you."

And I understand. For the first time in my life, I understand. She was with me always. It wasn't the end of her life when she left this earth, but just a change into a new one. Just like the daisy seed Grandpa buried into the earth. It transforms into a hidden new life as a flower.

I thought my mom abandoned me when she died—leaving me alone. But now I get it. She's been there all along: from my first steps walking to my first day of Kindergarten. As I look at the flash of my life before my eyes I see the movie version of my life (rated G, don't ya know). Mom is in the background of every scene. I watch, like a movie goer, and see how her influence has hovered around me.

She was there that day at the slide when the boy called me *prairie nigger*, and it was she who summoned up the courage deep down to hock the loogie on him. It was she who showed me how to tiptoe around when my dad was drinking.

And she is whispering in my ear to go back to a family member to understand why I feel the urge to say the weird things that come in my visions. Finally!

Mom, talk to me! What do these visions and questions mean?

Suddenly I leave the dream world as quickly as I entered it. The cool dampness of my surroundings sinks in, making me shiver. Slowly my eyes open and blink. My ears make out that sound again.

BANG!

But this time it's accompanied by voices hovering above me. Am I dead? Is this heaven? Somehow, I thought it'd be warmer.

Sniff. Sniff. And smell better.

I thought it'd be cleaner, too. Scraping the surface next to me I feel dirt under my fingers.

I look up to a bright light. I can make out a person who is surrounded by a glow. Is it an angel?

I see a large hand coming towards me. A very large callused hand within inches of my face.

And I hear the sound again.

"Bang?" it says.

"AHHHH! Help!!! Help!" I shriek with all of my might. I'm kicking and screaming my head off.

"Crykie, Sheila, simmer down or the shrimp'll be jumpin' off da barbie!"

That's no angel! Or even a gunshot! I'd know that voice anywhere.

Peeking over the edge above me are four dark faces peering down. Peering at me, who, seems to be in a grave. An empty grave (thank heaven for small favors).

"Junior! Help me out of here!" Tears of fear and joy run down my face as it's tilted upward, and I grab for his massive outstretched hand.

I get to a kneeling position and glance up again at my saviors. It's Junior who is smiling wildly, my grandparents, and of course, Little Nezzie.

"Apple, bang?" she says eating a piece of fry bread, letting the crumbs fall down into the grave on top of me. Her curls spill over the side of the top of my earthen tomb as she leans over casually, as if she's peering at fish swimming in a pond.

She reaches over the edge of the grave and asks again with outstretched hand, "Bang?"

Hearing her say that, I remember that was the sound I heard after the altercation with Rafe. Raising my hand, which is still clutching my necklace, and looking around my body, I see that there are no bullet holes. Rafe didn't shoot me after all.

So, it wasn't a gunshot I heard saying "bang," but Nezzie, once again, wanting to share her baeng, her fry bread. Of course, it doesn't help that she says it so LOUD! I must have blacked out from the fall into the grave.

Finally able to stand, I reach up to the giant paw of a hand Junior is extending to me. He lifts me out in one grand swoop. As soon as I step back on solid ground my family rushes to embrace me, tripping over themselves to get to me first.

Dazed and confused I ask, "W-what happened to me? How did I get in this g-grave? And WHAT happened to Karl's kid?"

Chapter 23

BACK DOWN IN THE parking lot my family begins to fill me in on what exactly happened that morning when I was "incommunicado" (i.e., six feet under). They were all tending the gravesites when Junior and Nezzie got hungry. Actually, they both thought the women back making lunch at the church would let them sneak a taste of the food they were making.

Assuming they'd find me back at the church they all decided to call it a day and head downhill. Only when they got there they couldn't find me. Then they walked to the back (only after, Nezzie told me, she and Junior did a "walkabout" through the kitchen to grab fry bread).

Mooshum looked outside the back door and noticed that the medicine wheel garden, the one where Rafe and I had our standoff, was completely trampled. When Grandma saw this, they looked at each other and, with me nowhere to be seen, sensed trouble.

Tearing off from the church's back door, Junior led the pack with everyone else following closely behind. They bounded up the path knowing they'd find me as they heard Rafe yelling at me.

Junior was the first to crest the hill. He saw Karl's son edging in closer to me, and he saw me jab Rafe in the elbow and fly around him again, leaping into space. I must have hit my head when I fell into the grave and it knocked me out.

Just as the rest of my family reached the top of the hill they witnessed my grand leap.

Grandpa grabbed Rafe's hunting rifle, and Junior pinned his arms back. Grandma ran back down the hill to call the police. Nezzie informs me, in a whisper, that she kicked Rafe . . . "where the sun don't shine." Teamwork is what it's really all about, people.

Amazingly this only takes place within a matter of minutes, but to me it was a lifetime. My lifetime. You might call me crazy (and you wouldn't be the first), but looking back now, I can honestly say that I'm slightly grateful for what Karl and his kid did to me. It took me a few days to feel this way, though, after the shock wore off.

I said you might think I'm crazy. But hear me out. Before this happened I was afraid, petrified, to go visit my mom's grave — any grave. My kookum, my grandma, is forever saying that everything happens for a reason. Rafe drove me, like a team of wild horses, up the path to see my mother. Karl's kid, in his weird twisted way, gave me my mother.

Don't get me wrong, he broke the law and will have to pay for that, and there is also a moral debt he will have to repay. But out of a tragedy came a blessing. If not for his actions, I would never have seen my mother, my most gracious advocate, who showed me through my dreams where she has been all my life. Right beside me all along. I just needed to open my heart to see it.

One of the police officers just happened to be preparing for funeral traffic control down the road from the church, so within seconds after Grandma called 911 we had backup. 10-4, good buddy.

While all this was happening, Junior ran over to the edge of the grave, my grave, and reached down to pull me up. Wait, isn't that ironic? Me, an Indian taking over and occupying land that I didn't own, and settling in, claiming it for a while . . . even if it was a grave? Sorry, settler-land-stealing sidebar.

Little Nezzie stuck close to Junior and in her own little way offered the best of what she had — bread, fry bread, baeng. Of course, my neurotic self heard *BANG*!

Don't judge me people unless you've lain in a grave before your time. You, too, might misinterpret what you see and hear. And you know what? Spending some quality time in that grave makes me realize that cemeteries aren't that bad of a place. Come to think of it, they're actually a place of life. Just a different life that we can't see. I think I'll still tip-toe through them, though, and think light thoughts.

* * *

A large round of hugs follows. Grandma and Grandpa have the paramedics, who were called by the police, check me out at the gravesite to make sure I am safe and sound. I'm a bit shaken, but surprisingly, not too bad.

As the tribal police lead Rafe away in handcuffs he stops, turns back and holds my gaze, but it's Karl who speaks "I . . . he never . . . never meant you no harm. It's . . . you . . . look so much like her . . . my mind got mixed up and I, Rafe, never would have harmed or stolen from you — "

"Karl, that's enough for today," Grandma interrupted. Then she turns away from me and says something to him quietly. It must have been powerful because he looks at her and nods solemnly, but I can't make out what she said.

"Grandma, what did you say to him?"

"Say? Well, I asked him 'isn't your wife allergic to daisies?'" And she tilts her head as she looks at me.

Oooo-kay.

"So, not to be rude, but what does that have to do with anything?"

"See, Apple, sometimes questions help people see better. See themselves better, more clearly. And, dear, Karl needs that desperately right now. He'll also have to help his son see himself better too."

Nodding in agreement, I answer, "I get that, but what's the deal with daisies?"

"Karl's wife's favorite flowers are roses, red ones if I remember right."

And she lip-points over my shoulders. She and I are the only ones still on the cemetery hill. The rest have followed the police back down to the church. I look again at her just as she smootchie-lips one more time. I turn my head to see what she's referring to. Just in back of me is the fresh grave I fell into. So, following her lip-pointing, I make my way back to the open grave and think that maybe I left something back there (like my dignity).

Standing right in front of it, I peer down to see what she's talking about. As I turn to ask her she's gone. Back down the path to the church, I'm assuming. I'm just about to head back myself. But glancing to the left of the grave I fell into I see it. Now I know what she was pointing to.

It's my mother's grave. And it's three feet from me. I cradle my head in my hands, and draw in a breath. It's the breath from deep within my soul, and I go to see my mother.

Her grave marker is a humble one. It's made of speckled black and gray marble with a simple memorial carved into its face. It reads:

Marion Bernadette (St. Pierre) Starkington

1968–1996

Here lies a beautiful soul.

Wife, mother, daughter, friend, teacher.

Just under her name is a flower. I bend to take a closer look and I can see that it's a picture of a daisy etched in the stone. A daisy? But that's what Grandma said to Karl. And that was also in the little garden lesson Grandpa told me. She so will be explaining the weird question thing she did back there. And now, I touch my gold necklace my dad gave me and understand what it meant: there is a small engraved daisy on the front. Did Karl think this necklace would bring my mom's love to him? Is this what he wants back? But my dad gave this to me.

My head is turning back and forth trying to figure out, no, trying to piece together the connection between what my grandma said. As my head glances back to the open grave where I fell, I notice something for the first time and it redirects my thoughts. My mom's grave is to the left of where I was when I fell in to get away from Rafe. It's to my *left*.

In my dream just a few hours ago, my mom was always to my left, and her kiss was even placed on my left cheek. Which means it truly was my mom who came to me in my grave-side dreams! It wasn't just me having some weird blackout unconscious hallucination — it was my mother helping me, telling me that she was with me my entire life, and she was with me when I fell six feet under. To my left.

* * *

It's so quiet up here, so peaceful. The lone sounds are a few cardinals and chickadees playing their songs. A few weeks ago, I asked Grandpa why my mom was buried up here in North Dakota instead of in Minnesota. After all, I said, my dad and I were in the Minneapolis metro area. Why wasn't she down there in Minnesota?

Grandpa answered that at the time my mom died, my poor dad just couldn't take it. He was so grief-stricken that it pained him to even admit that my mom died. He asked my grandpa if Mom could be buried back in the Turtle Mountains, her beloved home. Dad knew that the relatives, my relatives, could take better care of my mom up here.

And it looks like they did.

I know it may sound macabre, or even creepy, but I do something next that I've always dreamed of doing. I lay down next to her headstone, with my mother, and drift off to a soul-cleansing sleep. For those of you who have mothers, you take for granted something as simple as cuddling with her and taking a nap. This is my own version of resting with my mom.

Rest in peace, Mama, rest in peace.

Chapter 24

OF COURSE, WORD GETS back to my dad and Judy about this whole incident. And they decide to cut short their honeymoon. Who ever heard of a two-month honeymoon anyways? Why do they feel the need to be away from us kids so long? What's not to love about us? Whatever. They call to say they're picking up Baer from Judy's parents and will head up here.

Baer had been texting me the entire summer telling me all of the "adventures" he's been on with his grandparents. Let's see, first he said they made up some care packages, again. Only this time it wasn't to aid starving people in Africa; instead it was to help harbor seals off the coast of Alaska.

Apparently, Mae and Jed Silver, Jude's parents, had some concern (remember, her parents are kind, but kinda kooky) that the seals wouldn't be able to survive the frigid temperatures that far north. So, Baer learned to knit. He knit sweaters for the seals. I guess you could call them faux sealskin, or is it seal pup ponchos? Purl one, knit two.

These are seals, I texted back, that have inches of blubber to insulate against the cold. All Baer replied was, "I know. I know." I could hear his sigh of humiliation through the text.

The latest project was interrupted by the Karl craze. Baer texted me one sentence about it: We're raking up acorns. For the squirrels. To help with their winter stock.

Poor Baer, he really does put up with a lot. After all, he's put up with me all these years.

The evening after all the cemetery stuff happened, Grandma insists that I go get checked out at the hospital.

"We'll take you, Mooshum and me."

"But, I'm fine," I implore, not wanting to get prodded and poked.

"Eh, bien, then go for my sake. Nezzie and Junior will go pick some juneberries for you to have when you get back."

"Weeellll, all right." I so love my berries.

We head to Belcourt to the Indian Health Service building. Its façade is covered in brick and stone cut from a local quarry. That's another thing I noticed up here—that in the Turtle Mountains people use what they have. They use local materials. Back home in Minnesota some people on Lake Minnetonka ship in Carrara marble from Italy, or French porcelain tiles, even flying in exotic Zebra wood from the African continent to include in their houses. But to me, this makes more sense; it's more meaningful to use home-grown building materials.

Oh. My. Gosh. I sound like a granola-loving tree hugger.

In the waiting room there are about six people ahead of me. One by one they nod at my grandparents. And then they do the unimaginable. They nod to me! They actually nod to me and acknowledge my existence. I am Apple, hear me roar.

The nurse finally calls my name and I follow her back to the examining room. Don't you always peek into the little rooms you pass? I always do, too. In one room is a mom holding her baby on her lap as the nurse prepares to give the little one a shot. Down the hall I peer into another room (OK, so I pushed the door open a bit) and I hear the dad saying, "Well, I know I saw somethin' up your nose, and it wasn't no piggy bank I saw." The old "penny-up-the-nose" toddler trick. Yikes.

I'm so immersed in my hospital room observations that I almost lose the nurse ahead of me. She has bright red hair, so it's easy to catch up to her.

"Now, take a seat in here. I'll take your vitals before the doctor gets here."

Please don't tell me to get into one of those hospital gowns. They have no back to them and I have no self-respect in them either.

The nurse continues to look at my chart. And at me. Then down to my chart again. She brushes her flame-red locks out of her eyes and stares at me.

That *hair*. What is it about her hair?

We are in a staring match for a few seconds.

"Let's see here . . . umm," she says looking at her chart. "It says here your name is . . . Apple? Is that correct? It's not a typo, is it? Sometimes that front office doesn't know— "

"Yep," I interrupt her, "it's Apple all right. I guess I'm supposed to get checked out?" We're still in a staring mode, but we're pretending that all is well and normal (if she only knew who she was dealing with).

The nurse continues to flip her chart papers. And then she stops and sucks in her breath.

"Oh! Oh my word! You . . . you're . . ." nurse-whose-head-is-red says.

"Apple, remember?" Jeez, am I on the Alzheimer's unit?

And then it hits me. I know that face. That hair, I know, too!

I yell, "You're the one in the picture with my mom!

She yells, "You're Marion's daughter!"

I yell, "The picture from high school graduation — it's you!"

She yells, "I'd know your face anywhere! I knew someday I'd meet you!"

The doctor chooses that exact moment to walk in the door, and he hears us yelling and hugging and crying. He slowly ducks his head and backs out. Wise man.

* * *

I come to find out the nurse's name is Tiffany. She and my mom were best friends growing up and all throughout high school. Tiffany isn't Indian, but moved to the Turtle Mountains with her family when she was five. On the first day of first grade she and my mom were assigned desks next to each other and from then on, she says, they were inseparable.

When my mom went to North Dakota State University in Fargo to study teaching, Tiffany went to University of Minnesota to pursue a degree in nursing. She did her clinical studies at the Mayo Hospital, and then was offered a job back up in Belcourt, North Dakota, on the Turtle Mountain reservation. They lost touch for a bit after my mom and dad got married.

Cradling my face, she whispers, "Oh, I have thought about you so many times. It's just been so long. I didn't know you were up here. Which is surprising since word travels fast up here. Some call it gossip, but we call it the moccasin telegraph. For some it's the national pastime up here."

"I've been up here since June, spending time at my grandpar — I mean my mooshum and kookum's house. I even get to sleep in Mom's bedroom!"

"Oh my stars. We spent so many hours in her room planning about our future. She always wanted to teach, your mom. Marion was like the Pied Piper when it came to kids. They just flocked to her. She would always try to get me to teach Sunday School with her, but I just never had the knack."

We talk in that little room for what must have been close to an hour. She talks and tells me so many stories about my mom as she gives me the OK. I'm fit as a fiddle. Funny, the doc never does come back in to see me. That's America's health care system at its best.

We make plans to meet for lunch early next week. But as I hold the door to leave, one thing about her story comes back to me.

"Tiffany?'

"Yeah, Apple?"

"Did you say you did your clinicals for a few weeks at the Mayo? The hospital in Rochester, Minnesota?

"Yes, why?" She looks at me in a serious way. We both know what was coming.

"So, Tiffany, when was that?" I try to sound nonchalant.

"Well, let's see. It took me about seven years to get through college. I wasn't a brain, like your mom. I had to work twice as hard as everyone just to make it through."

Trying to keep her focused I continue, "And did you have any *memorable* cases when you were there at the Mayo Hospital?"

Her hand rips the door from my grasp and slams the door shut.

"Yes, I did! There was a case; I would have given everything I had to avoid it." Tiffany hides her face from me as she hugs me, burying her mass of red curls in my face.

"It was on a Friday. Late Friday night with the season changing from fall to winter. Highway 52, just outside of the city of Rochester, is notorious for car accidents. It's just a little road with no overpasses, so if people need to cross it, they gun it and try to speed up before an on-coming car hits them." Tiffany looks at me, gauging whether to continue. She can't sense if I'm ready to hear, so she pauses.

"Please," I beg, "it's time I know. You were there when my mom died."

"You're right, Apple. It's about your life, too, isn't it?"

Then for another few minutes she tells me of how the fog and icy rain had made traveling that night treacherous, but my mom wanted to stop by the Mayo Hospital where my dad was performing a last-minute surgery. She noticed earlier that he didn't bring his wallet, and she knew he'd be famished after the operation, so she piled into the car, eight months pregnant, and drove to bring it to him so he'd have money.

Only she never made it. A car, trying to cross the highway, spun out and hit her head on. She never saw it coming. It happened close enough to the city that within minutes an ambulance picked her up and had her to the emergency room quickly. The EMTs later told my dad that they didn't understand what my mom was saying. It seems she had already begun the travel back to her Native first languages: French and Michif.

Mom was brought to the same hospital where my dad was working that night. For the first time in his life, he was the loved one waiting to hear word of a family member hanging on to life with a thread.

Tiffany then tells me so many details about the operation in which the doctors tried to stop Mom's internal bleeding, but the trauma from the car crash was too much for her.

"You were one of the nurses with her in the operating room, weren't you?"

Tiffany nods without saying a word, keeping her face turned to the floor.

I'm remarkably calm considering this is the first time I'll know, really know what happened those last few moments of her life.

But I do hear one new thing my dad never mentioned before. Tiffany reminds me of last words coming from Mom's mouth.

"From what I can remember of that day, your mom said something like, '*Ma fille, la pomme de mes yeauxs*,'" That's a rough translation in French for: *My girl, the apple of my eye*.'" And that's how I got my name.

Yet I never knew what my mom said before that. Much before. Remember, this all happened within eleven minutes. In only eleven minutes, Mom was wheeled into the operating room and I was born. Tiffany tells me that the doctors said they were able to save my mother. They would need to give a high dose of narcotics and blood thinners to ease the pressure on the circulatory system. By administering this "cocktail," as they called it, my mom could get through the trauma done to her body.

"So, you're saying, my mom had a chance to live? Why hasn't anyone told me? Should we find those doctors and sue them? Come on!"

"Apple, Apple, let me finish, sweetie. See, there was just one caveat—it would adversely affect the baby in utero." Looking at me she finishes, "if she was to live, it would cause you to die, to have never seen the light of day."

"I . . . but . . . I don't understand why she . . . I mean she never even knew me, and she," I can't even finish my thought. The horrible thought that my mom, my lovely mother could have lived, and I caused her to die. It really is true. "I killed my mother."

I feel arms holding me tightly. Tiffany looks me square in the face, her eyes reaching and piercing years of misunderstanding.

"Oh, sweetie, no! You have it all wrong! Your mama, she knew you from the moment she found out she was pregnant. And loved you every day. But let me finish the story, Apple. After the doctors gave her that choice she never hesitated a moment. She looked at the doctor, and then to me, noticing that it was me, her childhood friend, pleading, she said to me, "Please. The baby must live. I *insist*."

"But I thought Mom spoke French her last few moments? How would the doctors have known what she said?"

"You're right, she was speaking one of her first languages, but when it really counted her soul was strong enough to come back lucid for the few seconds she gave the order to save you in English, so the doctors would understand."

"And that's when she named me, right? Wait—Tiffany, you weren't the nurse who took that to mean my name was supposed to be Apple, were you?"

"Oh, no, it was another nurse, but she was a good woman, and I truly think that we all saw how your mom looked at you and how joyful her laugh was as she said, '*Ma fille, la pomme de mes yeauxs*.' *My girl, the apple of my eye*. How could I argue with that, even though it may have been a mangled French interpretation?"

"You're right. It's the name Mom gave me."

We speak for a few more minutes, and then because I know she has a full day with appointments, I leave.

Back out in the waiting room, Grandma sees that Tiffany is walking me out and says, "Oh, I didn't know you were working today, Tiffany."

Yeah, right. Grandma knew all along why I needed to go to the doctor today. It was for healing all right, but a different kind.

Chapter 25

THE CAR RIDE HOME is interesting. I just keep looking sideways to my grandma, and she just hums along with the radio. Grandpa is driving and I see him glance at her as we open the truck doors, and she does a quick nod back. They were so in on this plan together.

They play dumb, and I can play that game, too. (Except most times I'm actually not acting.)

"So, thanks for taking me to the doctor. I feel *soooooo* much better now." (I know I should be more appreciative that they hooked me up with Tiffany, but, hey, I'm a teenager. Sarcasm is my middle name).

Actually, I never told you my middle name, did I? Well, maybe some other time. It's a doozy of a story, trust me.

"Grandma, I was meaning to ask you about that question you asked."

"Hmmm? What's that?"

"Remember, the one you asked Karl? Let's see . . . how did it go? Something like 'isn't your wife allergic to daisies?'"

Grandpa starts coughing up a storm. That's right; I'm on to their game. Grandma asking someone a weird question, one that comes out of nowhere? They both know something about my habit of asking questions.

"Spill it, toots." I say a bit too rudely. After a stern eye look from my grandparents I restate my question, "Umm, er . . . what I meant to say is: Grandma, I noticed that, just like I do, you asked someone a weird question. Why? The truth . . . please."

Grandma looks at me in the back seat and nods, "Yes, Apple. You're right. It's time for the truth. Let's me and you go for a walk when we get back home. Your father, Baer, and Judy are there already. I don't think they need to hear this."

With a wink, Grandpa adds, "Yep, my girl, it's high time you learn da family trait."

O.M.G. I'm a voodoo princess. That can be the only explanation. OK, so maybe not. It's the longest twenty minutes back home.

We come within sight of the house. I can see my dad's car there (and I hope it has aired out since the last time I was in it). Grandpa slows the truck down and lets Grandma and me off a few blocks away.

Side by side we walk for a few seconds without saying a word.

Then she turns to me, "Apple, my girl, you're right. We—no, I—should have told you this sooner. Much sooner. Right when I noticed that you had . . . *it* . . . too. Right after the time you told us you asked Karl a question at Dan's Truck Stop.

"It? What's *it*?"

"Your questions you ask. The ones that pop up in your mind? Do you sometimes see things in your mind before you blurt out the question?"

"Yes!" My eyes are riveted to her.

Smiling, she continues, "Well, that sounds about right. You, my girl, have the family gift. You have *it*."

Why do I think the clouds should part and the sun shine down its rays on me now? But no such luck.

"Apple, you are able to see the one aspect of a person's life that they are not living truthfully. The visions are a part of someone's life that is holding them back, something that they are not being honest about."

"Oh, OK, I sort of get that . . . yes! But, Grandma, what about the weird questions?"

"The questions are a way that shows the person the area in their life they are clinging to, holding on to something and treasuring it, but it's holding them back from being their true self. You said something to Karl, and to his son, to show them something."

"So, I sort of ask them the question, and the answer helps them to see themselves better? To know what they should get rid of?"

With an arm around me, she nods. "So tell me, who has this happened with?"

"Well, hmmm, let's see. I think it was my English teacher, Mrs. Katterwall. I had some weird image of her reading a comic book and I ended up asking her if she liked reading Calvin and Hobbes comics in the tub."

Grandma just looked at me, "And so?"

"And so, she is such a book snob always throwing around fancy books she reads . . . Oh! Oh! Grandma, I get it! My teacher likes reading comic books, and yet she lies about it and tries to cover up that fact by pretending to be a book snob." Can you see the light bulb turning on over my head, or what? "Why doesn't she just figure that out for herself?"

"For some reason, Apple, so many people bury their true selves deep in their heart. Our family, the ones who have this ability, help others to get back to the person they were created to be. We don't brag about this ability, we don't gossip about it. It is a great responsibility."

"I understand, Grandma. So, who in our family has this?"

"Oh, it's not for me to tell other people's stories. I can tell you that I have it, but just a touch. And, your mama had it. She was so gentle about the way she approached people." Looking at me she continues, "And maybe you should tone it down, just a bit. People are more apt to take medicine if it's sweet."

And we talk about the other times I've had this happen to me and what it means.

Although she couldn't figure out what it meant when I said, "Eye ate teen" to Marcia the "Two-fer" mean girl back at school in Minneapolis.

Man, if I had only known. My life would have been so much easier. But, I guess, in a way, my crazy wacked-out questions are meant to help people. Somehow, I am a part of a plan, like Mooshum told me this summer. I needed to figure out what I was meant to do in life. Helping people seems like an honest start.

But as we edge closer to Grandma's house there's one more interpretation I need to talk about. One more thing that needs to be aired out.

"Karl. I asked Karl and Rafe twice something about the singer Barry Manilow. Seriously, how can that help him to dig out what is untruthful in his life? Barry Manilow—the easy-listening singing legend?"

"Think, my girl. Why do you think this a question that he needed to hear? What was it that he was not being true to?"

And then it hits me like a ton of bricks, or actually like a ton of mixed cassette tapes. For all of you too young to remember, back before iPods and even CDs there were cassette tapes that you could record music to. Apparently, Karl must have recorded a bunch of Barry Manilow tunes to a tape and given it to my mom. That's what he was talking about when he cornered me at Dan's Truck Stop. Something about "my mama owes him" something. And since she wasn't here I'd have to give it back or give him money, or my necklace. A tape? A music tape circa 1980? Are you kidding me? All he wanted was the mix tape of Barry Manilow music he made for my mom? Whew. What's the deal with Barry? I ask Junior later and he reels off a boat load of greatest hit tunes by Mr. Manilow: "The Copacabana," "I Write the Songs," "Mandy," and "Can't Smile Without You."

"But, Grandma, really, how could asking Karl about a mixed tape help him see the one area in his life that he's not being honest? And why did he think it was worth a lot of money?"

"See, Apple, the one who has the vision and knows the questions to ask is really the one who needs to interpret it. What is it about that tape that Karl needs to get over?"

I look at her and know. It's simple.

"He needs to get over my mom. Maybe he really opened himself up when he made the Barry Manilow mixed tape, and when my mom rejected him, he didn't want anyone else to know that he opened his heart to someone." Now I remember the box of tapes under my mom's bed. One of them must have been the tape he made for my mom. The one with flowers and hearts drawn all over it. The one he didn't want anyone to know about. The one that wasn't worth any amount of money, just his pride.

Grandma kisses me on the cheek and whispers, "I think you've got it. And the question I asked him about the daisies?"

Smiling, I answer, "Daisies were my mom's favorite flowers, weren't they? I saw a picture of them on her gravestone and my necklace. Karl needed to be reminded of his wife's favorite flower. But really, Grandma, the question helped him to remember that he has a wife, and it isn't my mom."

"Right on, pukkon." This is Grandma's favorite saying. What is it with this family and food references? First, it's Aubergine (a.k.a eggplant) and then there's Apple—what's next? Cousin Raisin? Uncle Cashew?

Chapter 26

TO THE FRONT STEPS we walk arm in arm. My family is on the front deck. This is sort of funny, because the first time I arrived up here I was so intimidated by the relatives on the deck. In my mind they were strangers. And now?

They're all here, but this time my Minnesota family is mixed in among them. Auntie Auber is on the rocking chair next to my dad. She's leaning over whispering something to him and his head is rolling back in laughter. Judy has Little Nezzie on her lap and is braiding her hair. Nezzie is singing her newest song from preschool, "*Head, shoulders, knees, and toes.*" I can hear Judy singing along, but of course when she says "s" it comes out like a high pitched "sssssssssssssssss." Nezzie stops and looks up at her, trying to figure out where that whistling sound is coming from, but continues on with her song. Am I the only one who thinks Judy's sibilant s is a riot? I know, I should respect my elders, but I am who I am.

And there on the steps are Junior and Baer debating just who the MVP will be this year: someone from the Cubs, or the Minnesota Twins (yeah, right). Junior holds out his sausage-sized finger saying, "Pull it." Ugh. Boys — are they always obsessed with gas? Oh, Lord, Baer is actually going to yank it.

"Hi!" I yell running through the front yard.

Chairs screech as everyone gets up. This time everyone gets up.

Judy and my dad run down the steps first.

"Why, honey, you've . . ."

"Oh, Apple, look at you . . ." Dad says.

I look down and imagine how I must look to them. They haven't seen me for weeks, actually two months and six days to be exact. The jeans I'm wearing are just plain Levi's — my mom's Levi's. I've got her cowboy boots on, and my hair is grown out and not even done today. Let's just gloss over the issue of my extra fifteen pounds I've gained and the fact that I haven't used a drop of sunscreen since I got here. I'm as tan as tobacco (Nicorette aside).

"I know, I know. I must look horrible."

At the same time Dad and Judy gasp, "Oh, sweetie, you look . . . beautiful!"

We all go back inside the house and catch up on this summer. Grandma and Auntie set out quite a spread for dinner.

Nezzie is spewing crumbs out of her mouth as she lifts up her offering to Judy and says (again), "Bang? Bullets?" I look at Junior as we see Judy take a second look trying to make sense of what's going on. We're all feasting as if we hadn't eaten in ages. I think joy makes a person hungry.

Mooshum is pointing out to Baer which plate has the venison ribs on it and which has the beef spare ribs. Of course, my fearless brother takes a hunk of Bambie and proclaims it, "Awesome!" Gross. I prefer the spare ribs and finish off two of them.

"How'd ya like da spare ribs, my girl?"

"Mmmm, really good, Grandpa. Maybe next time I'll actually try your deer meat." Sure, I will.

"Well, no time like da present."

"No, thanks. I don't do deer."

Why is everyone smiling?

"Well, my girl, I may have forgotten to put da spare ribs out dis time," he says with fake innocence.

I. Think. I. Just. Threw. Up. A. Little. In. My. Mouth. Thumper, Flower, please don't hate me. I just ate deer.

"Ha, ha, everyone. Laugh at my expense. If I were you all, I'd sleep with one eye open tonight." I can't believe I just ate Bambi.

It's the best of times. It's the first best of times I've ever had.

The next two days are filled with nonstop talking and laughing and Judy being freaked out by minor things (going to the "old place" to feed Mooshum's horses and she has to use an outhouse, picking juneberries in the bush and having to literally comb wood ticks out of her hair. Good times, good times.)

My dad and I get a rare chance to ride alone on a trip to pick up some supplies. We're going through a lot of food with everyone here and a lot of toilet paper with my brother, Baer, here. Don't even ask.

The next day Auntie Auber gets word and tells us that Rafe is sentenced to two hundred hours of community service. I may have shown up to his sentencing hearing and explained a few things. Karl and Rafe just looked at me and nodded. So did Karl's wife. I'm still not happy about what Rafe did to me, but I need to move on. Junior has a quote he's always saying, "Any fool who can make you angry has control of your life."

Nobody is going to control my life anymore, only me.

* * *

That night we all sleep again at Grandma's. She insists my parents stay in their house. (Did you catch that? I called Judy "my parent"! It has a nice ring to it. Notice I also don't call it a trailer anymore? Love makes a home, and this one is bursting at the seams with it.)

Nezzie sleeps on one couch and I sleep on the other one so Judy and my dad could take my bedroom . . . er, my mom's bedroom. Well, the extra bedroom. I tuck Nezzie in after we say prayers. I sort of like her version of the bedtime prayer better:

Now I laid me down to sleet;
I pray da Lord my sold to keep.
If I should lie before I take
I pray da Lord my sword to tape.

I pull up the blankets and put them under her chin, and as I kiss her cheek I whisper, "Good night."

Turning to walk back to my couch, I hear her whisper back, "Goodnight to you, my girl."

Awwww. Ain't' she sweet?

And as I'm drifting between this world and the dream world, I feel someone climb in with me. Nezzie. She whispers again into my ear, "Apple, what's with da gold in gate?"

"Hmmmm? What?" lazily I respond, my eyelids heavy with sleep.

"Da gold in gate? What's dat, Apple?"

"Hmmmm?" I answer in the haze of slumber.

"Da gold in gate, Apple? What's dat?"

"I don't know, now it's time for bed. You can sleep with me as long as you're quiet."

And we both sleep the deep sleep of peace.

I wake up the next morning to Mooshum cooking in the kitchen and doing a mighty fine jig. Nezzie must be in there already. I feel something on my forehead and flick it off (I may have a slight bug phobia). When I peek down on the floor to see what it is, I see it's a tiny plastic turtle about half an inch long. I notice the window above the couch has been left open all night. But Karl wouldn't come around here, would he? Did Rafe? Maybe it's Karl's other boys continuing the threats? What does this turtle mean?

Chapter 27

IT'S SUNDAY THE NEXT morning, and so the frenzied family is tripping over each other as we get ready for church.

Being the last one to use the bathroom, I'm trying to do something with my hair. The walls are pretty thin in this place, and so I can hear my dad and Judy talking in my mom's bedroom. (OK, so I may have put my ear up to the wall, but you didn't hear that from me.)

"It'd be good for you, Ed. You know that."

My dad sighs, "I know, Judy, you're right. It's been so long since we've been to church, but I guess today would be a good day to start again. I've forgotten about the strong Native American spiritual heritage. There's a strong connection to God, the Creator, or I guess whatever name you use." He pauses, "As we drove up you mentioned how run down, how poor, the reservation looks. But, Judy, I think they may be the wealthy ones of the world. The rest of us have a poverty of spirit because our heart gets cluttered with always trying to get more: more money, more awards, more . . . stuff that suffocates our lives."

"Yes, I think you just may be right, dear. And after the service?" Judes prods.

"And after, Judy, I want to visit her." He pauses. "It's been so many years. I realize I've made such a mistake by not talking about her to Apple. If I could just redo — "

"Hindsight is always twenty-twenty. Apple has had such a good time up here. And it's good for you to be up here, too."

I hear a sickening smack that sounds like a kiss. Gross. Parental PDA — worse than seeing them attempt to dance. At least I just heard them kiss and didn't have to witness live and in 3D.

"How was I lucky enough to find you? How do you put up with me?" Dad whispers.

"Because your paycheck makes up for the rest of you."

I could hear both of them laughing. I guess Judy does make my dad happy. How did I miss that before?

"And, Judy . . . after the service . . . I'd like you to come up to see her, too. I know she would have loved you," Dad says.

We all pile into Grandpa's truck. We kids get to ride in the truck bed. With no seats. With no seatbelts. Man, this is fun! I can see Judy constantly looking back at us to make sure we don't fly out. There is nothing like cruising down the highway of life with no cares but the wind in your face. (Note to self: do not talk in back of truck when it's going over fifty-five; keeping the bugs out of your mouth is high priority.)

As we get closer to St. Francis Xavier Church, we pass by the reservation sign. And once again it has graffiti spray painted that neon green.

This time it says: "You're *NOT* Welcome to the Turtle Mountain Chippewa Indian Reservation." Karl's kid is at it again. Junior just looks at me and shakes his head. Nezzie copies Junior, shaking her head, too, and makes a sour face with her lips.

I guess some people just never get over their hatred. A few days after that incident with Karl at Dan's Truck Stop I remember asking Grandpa why one Indian person was being a jerk to another Indian. I (foolishly) thought we all were supposed to stick together. Grandpa got a far-off look in his eyes and answered me with a story, which he did a lot.

"See, there was dis man I met after da war. I was stationed in Poland during da war, but didn't meet him until many years after. He was a Jewish man and spent da war in a German concentration camp. I'll never forget what he told me. In fact, he wrote a book about his experiences. You would tink he would be a bitter man. After all, he lost most of his family in da camps and da Nazis tried to take away his humanity. Yet, Viktor, dat was his name, said da one thing no one could take from his was his attitude; if you can find a reason to live, you can survive any trial or hardship. And dat you can basically split people, all people, into two races: dat of da decent, and dat of da indecent."

"So, Grandpa, you're saying that there will be jerks that are white and good people that are white, and jerks that are Indian and good people that are Indian?"

"Eya."

A pat on my head confirmed that I got it right. Just because Karl and his kids are Indian, my race, my peeps, doesn't automatically mean that they'll respect or accept me. How unfortunate.

As we pull into the church parking lot, I think how nice it is for my family, both sides of my family, to be together. We all walk into the church and take up two pews toward the front (Baer had a laughing fit when he heard Junior say, "go sit in the pew up dere."

Baer thinks anything sounding remotely stinky is hilarious. OK, I laugh, too.)

Some people nod at my dad like they know him. I never really thought about that; that my dad has been up here before. It's almost like he had a whole life before I came along.

The church service is nice. Afterwards I head to the kitchen with Grandma to make lunch. She says if I want to learn how to make fry bread I need to practice, practice, practice. I stay there with her and Auntie Auber. I want to respect my elders, so I take orders how to "dice like this" and "stir like that." Dad and Judy go up to visit Mom's grave. Junior and Baer head out back to talk sports.

And Little Nezzie is out in the parking lot and playing with sidewalk chalk. She begged Mooshum this morning to bring her bike, her "ride," as she calls it, so she'd have something to do while the rest of us women cook after church. I see her run over to Jeff in the parking lot, can hear her asking for just "a little song," but he pats her head as he walks by and says something about a possible job at the Casino playing guitar on the weekends. She just throws her arms around him and runs off to ride her bike. Kids. They'd forgive you for just about anything.

I think I laugh more than I had ever with Auntie Auber in the kitchen. She says things like, "Apple, you want a man to notice you? Make sure you remember one ting: to overlook da hair in his nose." Or my favorite: "My girl, if you tink a guy is 'da one,' see if he knows his mama's birthdate. If he does, grab him, because if he treats his mama good, he'll treat you good, too! If not, let him walk da plank."

I just stand for a minute and take in everything. For the first time in my life I feel happy and content. It's a moment to savor. Because it won't last.

Chapter 28

I DON'T REMEMBER WHO hears it first. I think it first rings my ears as I'm taking a break from doing the dishes back in the kitchen. It sounds like a mosquito in my ear at first, and then I notice Grandma stopping what she's doing and tilting her head up. Then Auntie does the same, along with all the others. We all turn to face the music.

A siren. A loud siren screams in the distance. As in any emergency you check on your loved ones. I see Dad and Judy running down the hill. Check. Through the same window I catch a glimpse of Grandpa working back in the garden. Check. Baer and Junior are running through the kitchen. Check, check.

But one person is missing. My Nezzie. My best friend. *My girl.*

Now I've never been a mother, but when a little one is missing your whole mind reacts like it's in slow motion. I run out to the parking lot. I'd just seen her racing around on her bike.

"Nezzie!" I scream. "Nezzzzzzie! Where are you?"

Everyone splits up and searches the church, the yard, and up the hill to the cemetery.

She is nowhere. But the siren keeps getting louder and louder. Drowning out even the bird songs that are so prevalent up here.

Junior has his cell phone out and is already connected to his friends on the county EMT crew. He looks at all of us, then puts his head down and looks away; refusing to make eye contact and whispering so softly into his phone that none of us can hear him. Berta is next to him, murmuring something. They lock eyes, but all I see is fear bouncing between them.

"Junior!" I yell running towards him. "Tell me! Where is Nezzie? Where is Little Inez?"

My hands beat on my gentle giant. I know before I even ask him. I know. You recognize when the other half of your heart is gone.

His large arms surround me and won't let me go. Into his massive chest I let my tears stream down and mingle with the ground beneath us.

We find out that Nezzie had ridden her bike out of the church parking lot without any of us knowing. She always stayed close to us. She never strayed, but this time she wanted to do something for us. She wanted to make the world more beautiful for us.

Oh, my little one. If you only knew that you made our world more beautiful.

She rode out onto the highway, a busy highway, just down from the church to the sign. She peddled her bike to the Welcome to the Turtle Mountain Chippewa Indian Reservation sign that was constantly riddled with graffiti. Before she left the church parking lot Nezzie grabbed all of the white sidewalk chalk and was going to try to color over the bright green paint that we all disapproved of so much. It represented a seething hatred for another race, and even this little child knew when enough was enough.

Nezzie just wanted to make the world a lovelier place. Except she never got a chance to finish her masterpiece. A car full of teenagers, the driver who was texting, crossed over the center line and hit her at sixty miles an hour. She never even had a chance.

And again, I feel lost in the world. It's a sad place when your best friend, the one who never judged you, the one who loved you unconditionally, has suddenly left you to yourself. To fight the demons alone.

Chapter 29

HER FUNERAL IS TO be on Friday. We need a few days to try to find Big Inez, her mom. Surprisingly, Karl is the one who ends up locating her out in California. Not sure how he knew where to find her; not sure I want to know.

We meet the hearse outside of St. Francis Xavier's main door. The men carry Nezzie's coffin into the church. It's so little. And we stay with her all morning and all afternoon. Auntie Auber says that's tradition. Up here a family stays with the deceased relative, never leaving them alone. Sometimes they stay with the body all night if the funeral is the next day. Even in death, Indian people keep watch over those they love, never wanting them to be alone.

She died from a severe head injury to the back of her skull, but looking down at her it just looks like her eyes are closed. Nezzie's mom decides to have an open casket. To me, it seems that she doesn't have the right to make any choices in the funeral. But no one asks me. I can't go up to see my little girl at first during the viewing. But Judy takes my hand and we walk up and kneel before Nezzie. Sometimes you just need someone to help you find your courage. She looks so peaceful, just like she was asleep. Angel that she is.

I have to touch her one last time; to make sure that she really existed. There are a lot of people touching her, gently, so I know it's OK to do. I brush a curl away from her face and tuck it behind her ear. And as I did that I glance down to her feet. She has on her beautiful colorful beaded moccasins with the floral design. It's the same Ojibwe floral design that's everywhere up here in the Turtle Mountains.

It makes sense to me to bury a loved one in their moccasins. I guess it symbolizes their journey to the next life. But what do I wear back here to walk my path in life without my best friend?

There is a steady drizzle with fog surrounding the little church. How fitting. The earth seems in a haze without her, too. Cars fill the church's parking lot, with overflow room on the road in front of the building. The whole town turns out. But it doesn't matter how many people come. There's only one person missing here. I miss my friend, my cousin.

Dad, Judy, and Baer sit next to me in the second row during the funeral Mass. Big Inez sits in the first pew. I can't figure out how she could have left Nezzie — the child whose heart was so big. Later Auntie reminds me that some people can't see the gold before their eyes because they have addictions that we just don't understand.

The priest gives as good a funeral Mass as one can give for a child who died too young. Gathering our things after Father gives us the final blessing, we're getting ready to leave.

And then I hear it. The silence and the sobbing are interrupted as the first chord breaks through. It takes a few seconds for all of us to understand what's happening.

Gentle child, quiet sight,
Morning light so pure and bright,
Gentle child, lovely one,
You gave us laughter, gave us love.

Walking up the aisle with guitar in hand, serenading Little Nezzie, is Jeff. He looks only at her and sings a version of a gospel hymn in a solid wave of sadness. It's an incredible voice and now I know why my little girl tried to coax it out of him. This voice, this gift of his, is too important to keep to himself and that little girl knew it. He changed a church song to make it fit Nezzie perfectly. His gaze is intent, and he continues up the aisle until almost arriving at the casket, but stops next to me, and nods, our eyes holding each other's gaze for what seems like eons.

I know what he means. I can read his eyes and understand. He means, "I thought I never had time to sing to her before, but now I'll drop my entire life to serenade her and guide her on her path into the next life." Jeff sings a song for every year Nezzie was alive, and then goes and sits next to Mooshum.

There isn't a dry eye in the place. Once again, Little Nezzie brings down the house.

* * *

After the funeral, we walk up the hill to the cemetery. It's to an open grave we head. But this time, instead of me going in, it's someone else. But you might as well bury my heart in there, too. Funny though, I'm not afraid of going to a cemetery now. No, I realize that our loved ones, below ground, are mingling with the Earth, and as we lightly walk over their grave, our steps echo their heartbeat which remains with us, connecting us always.

The priest says a few Bible passages and then we're left there. Little Nezzie's coffin is so tiny—just pine planks, but it holds a princess. We watch as they lower her into the grave. One by one the relatives walk past and grab some dirt that's piled up off to the side and throw it in. A few bring little pink Turtle Mountain wild roses, and others bring wild sage to throw in. But even these sweet scents cannot cover the odor of grief.

Walking past her grave some say "goodbye." Some say "God bless you." Some say "Gigawabamin," which Grandma translates as "I will see you again" in the Ojibwe language. I don't understand, but she explains that in Ojibwe there is no word equal for "goodbye," and that's important to me, because I *will* see her again. Just not in this life.

It's my turn, so I grab a handful of dirt and sprinkle it over her, "I'll see you again, *my girl*." And I start to walk back down the hill along with the rest of the people. But I notice that Grandpa, Jeff, and Junior stay back. I look to Grandma to see what to do, and she's nodding to the grave. I know I'm supposed to stay. It's amazing how much you can learn by just watching. Even through silence, communication continues.

"Is there something more we need to say?" I whisper to Junior as we're left alone.

His lips point to the pile of dirt piled behind the open grave.

"What?"

Now his eyes point to the shovels leaning against the dirt mound.

"What do you mean?"

The men grab shovels and begin the unthinkable. They start to move the dirt from the pile back down over Little Nezzie.

"Wha—what are you doing?! You mean *we* bury her?" Looking around I add, "But doesn't the cemetery crew do that?"

Grandpa shakes his head. Junior holds out a shovel to me. Jeff continues to shovel.

"My girl," Mooshum speaks softly, "when you were a girl, who tucked you into bed at night?"

OK, he's WAAAY off topic.

"Who tucked me into bed? Well, I guess that would've been my dad, or Judy after they married. Sometimes a babysitter. What does that have to do with me shoveling dirt over . . . Ne-Nezzie?" My voice breaks as I say her name.

"So, relatives, family members put you to bed at night?" Grandpa asks just above a whisper.

I nod, with one eye on Junior as he slowly moves the dirt bit by bit into the tomb.

"Who better, Apple, den family to tuck our child into her eternal slumber?"

My body somehow moves the shovel to help. It's like a dream. This can't be real.

A few feet away from where Nezzie lies is my mother's grave. *Watch over her, Mom, in the next life; in heaven. Will ya?*

I grab the remaining shovel and begin to tuck Nezzie in with the soil of the Turtle Mountains. My tears covering Nezzie, and my sorrow blanketing her, too.

Chapter 30

WE'RE A SOLEMN CROWD the next few days. There's no *joie* in our *joie de vivre*. Dad and the rest of my Minnesota family start to help pack my things. It's time for me to leave. Summer is almost over. School will begin soon. Dad and Judy are discussing a possible last-minute trip. To get "our minds off of what happened." As if I can think of anything else.

I spend a lot of time in my mom's bedroom that last day, just wanting to absorb everything before I leave. Grandma and Grandpa already said we all could come back for Christmas. I ask if I could stay next summer, too. Of course, Baer tried to get in on that action. Actually, I might let him. He's starting to grow on me.

But there's one thing I still don't understand as I lie here on the bed. Across the room on the dresser are five little things arranged in a line. The things that someone gave me. Warnings or gifts.

First it was a jar of dirt. Then it was a small bag of wild sage. Next to that are the remaining presents: a feather, some juneberries, and finally I add the last object: a little plastic toy turtle. All of these are remnants of my Turtle Mountain time.

I must be in a daze because I don't even hear my dad come in. He sits on the bed next to me.

"Apple, sweetie, it's time to go. Are you ready?"

I look up to him. Where did those lines come from next to his eyes? Has he always had gray at his temples?

"Dad, I guess I'm ready. But . . ."

"But what?" He gently fingers my necklace. "I'm so glad to see you wearing that. It was your mother's. Did you know that?"

Somehow, I knew that without him even telling me.

Staring at the top of the dresser I say, "But Dad, I don't understand why someone gave me these things."

Dad gets up and walks over to look at my cache of gifts. He leans against the doorway, grabs the jar of dirt and twists the lid off. Carefully he pours some of the contents into his palm. My dad squeezes the soil letting it stay formed in a clump. Next, he takes out the sage, crumbles it gently in his hands and brings it to his face while he inhales its fragrant scent.

I watch my father do what seems the most mundane thing. He is, ever the medical man, investigating the mystery before him. Back in Minnesota watching my dad, the doctor, sort out his medical cases has always been a fascination of mine. If you looked at him close enough you were able to read his face while he debated against himself between the correct diagnosis and, in turn, the best path for treatment. Dad always incorporated all of his senses.

"That's it!" My head jerks up from the bed. "Dad! I've got it! I know what this means. I get why I got these things! AND I know who gave them to me!"

Dad's eyes glimmer a bit as he says, "Enlighten me." I look up to see everyone crowded around the bedroom door now, Judy and my grandparents. OK, so I have a loud voice. There could be worse things in life.

"The dirt," I say looking at everyone now in the room. "Oh, Dad, it was Nezzie! It was her all along — not Karl or Rafe! And it wasn't just a weird childish whim. These were never threats. They were gifts! This is the dirt, the soil, the feel of the Turtle Mountains. Next, the sage. It is the smell, the scent of the reservation."

Grandma is smiling, "Apple, I think you're on to something!"

Pacing back to the bed and around to the open window, I can hear the ever-present song of the birds out in the backyard. "And the feather — the sounds of it up here. The juneberries? The taste up here — the sweet taste of life up here. In fact, it's my favorite taste, and Little Nezzie knew that."

Dad picks up the little toy turtle and rubs its shell. "And this stands for the name of the Turtle Mountains?"

Grinning ear to ear I answer, "Nope, but close. It's the look of the land up here. The first thing I noticed driving up here was the change of the land and how it started sloping into gentle hills. Nezzie gave me this little gift," I take the turtle from Dad, "because the land up here looks like little turtle shells are underneath the grass."

Back and forth I look at my dad and Judy, and my grandparents. I'm not seeing the light bulbs going off over their heads yet. Grownups these days.

"OK, stay with me, you guys. Nezzie gave me what she already had. She knew that eventually I'd have to go back to Minnesota, so she made a little care package, Nezzie-style. I can't take all of the relatives back with me, and I can't take the Turtle Mountains with me. So, she gave me something from up here for every one of my senses to remember it all by: Taste: juneberries, touch: earth, hear: bird feather, smell: sage, and look: turtle."

Grandpa pats my head, "Well, I'd say you got dat just about right."

"It's . . . it's the nicest gift anyone has ever given me." My voice cracks at the thought of such a wise gift from such a tiny girl. Like they say, "and a little child shall lead them." And lead me she did: into finding where I came from. Which I desperately need in order to find out where I'm going in life.

I'm not happy about leaving, but I know that one's life must move forward. The thing that still bothers me was one of the last things Nezzie asked me the night before she died: "What's with the *gold* in *gate*?" Nobody seems to understand what that means either.

* * *

My bags are packed and I'm ready to go this morning. Everyone is outside waiting to leave. Taking everything in as I walk around the house, I breathe in the scent of Grandma's house. It seems to be one-part apple pie, one-part laundry detergent, and a sprinkle of coffee. But to me, it's the sweet smell of family.

On the front porch Junior, Auntie Auber, Berta, and my grandparents are hugging and saying their goodbyes. The rest of the Minnesota clan makes its way to the car while I force myself, one step at a time, to leave the place where I finally found myself.

Dad decides, right away this morning, that we all definitely need a quick vacation, me, Baer, Judy, and Dad. We need time, he says, to rest. Sounds good to me. But it'll take more than a vacation to heal my heart.

First, we need to say our goodbyes. Turning to Auntie I say, "Thank you so much for helping me with the dream interpretation."

Waving her arm, Auntie replies, "Eh bien, just make sure you practice makin' baeng at home. You're all too skinny."

Junior grabs me into a bear hug and lifts me off the ground. “You’ll be OK. I was worried about ya, city girl, but now I know . . . we made an Indian out of you. An odd one, but one dat no one will ever forget.” He adds a wink.

“Eh bien! Junior, we didn’t *make* her an Indian. She just had to find it, inside of her.” Grandma to the rescue. Wrapping me in her arms, she kisses me on both cheeks and whispers, “My girl, we love you. Remember that I’m just a phone call away if you need anything. Christmas vacation will be here before you know it.” Her hands gently cup my face as she gazes into my eyes one more time.

Mooshum feigns fixing the railing on the deck. I know he’s waiting until everyone moves to the car to say his goodbye to me.

“Apple, my girl, you are just da joy in my heart now. I am gonna miss you. Who’s gonna get up and eat with me so early in da mornin’?” Kissing me on the forehead he continues, “Now, you do well in school. Make us proud—try to figure out what you were meant to do in dis life.” Grandpa says, “We must ask: what was I created to do? What was I meant to do to contribute? And, Apple, be good to your dad and Judy—dey love you, too.”

Judy says to me as I step into the car, “Do you want front or back?”

Winking at Grandpa, I answer, “Hmmm? Oh, no thanks. I don’t like yak.” He smiles and winks back.

We pull out of the driveway and I can barely look back. In only a few short months I’ve had a lifetime of experiences: I got to know a whole new family, learned about my Indian side, figured out the meaning of my crazy questions, met Karl and Rafe and took a short “nap” down under, I finally met my mom, and I made and lost my best friend. I'd say I have a boat load of things to write about when school starts and the teachers assign the good ole' essay "What I Did Over Summer Vacation."

I force myself to look over my shoulder as Dad starts driving away. Everyone is in the driveway waving. Everyone in the car but me is waving back. I roll the window down (Baer was already smelling ripe).

I can see Berta as she slips her hand into Junior's. They're quite a sight to be seen: Humpty Dumpty and Skinny Minnie. Well, I guess that just goes to show that there's a Jack for every Jill, init? I wonder if I'll find the salt to my pepper, the pie to my apple. He kisses the top of her head and I hear him yelling, "Gigawabamin, see you again!"

A surge of emotions wells up in me as I yell back and wave like a mad woman, "Gigawabamin!" Yes, I'll see you again, my family, but I'll never say goodbye. Languages tell a lot about a culture, and the fact that the language of my relatives had no word for goodbye means that I'll never be alone again. In this life, or the next, I will be with them all.

The Land Rover makes its way down the street and out of Morinville, North Dakota. I know in my head we have to leave, but my heart is desperate to stay. My dad turns on the radio to fill the silent car. With my iPod on as loud as it can crank, I lean my head against the window and watch the gentle sloping turtle-backed hills pass me by.

As we round the curve to catch the highway south, I notice the sign. That sign. I have to twist to look back out the window, but there, next to the "Welcome to the Turtle Mountains" sign is Karl. It's the same spot where Little Nezzie died trying to make our world nicer.

I can't be sure, but it looks like one of his sons is there, too. It's Rafe. The one from that day at the cemetery — the one who always had the green spray paint.

"Dad, can you please, um, pull over? I need to do something."

"Did Baer puke already?!"

"No, quickly, Dad. I have to wrap up some loose ends."

Karl looks up for a split second and catches my eye. He nods solemnly.

Judy starts to protest as soon as she sees who is on the side of the road, but my dad puts his hand on hers and pats it. As the car slows to a stop, I dig around my purse and find it. I wrap my hands around it and step out of the car, holding onto the door, trying to balance my soul.

"Karl, I — "

"No. Stop. Don't . . ." Karl stammers while shaking his head gently back and forth. I look and notice he and Rafe are planting flowers around the sign.

"Here," I whisper, holding the object out to him as a peace offering, across the chasm of forgiveness.

"Oh, you didn't . . . you didn't need — "

"But I did. Take it and — "

He takes grabs the tape — *that* tape — the mixed taped he made for my mom with Barry Manilow love songs. It has flowery drawings all over it. Karl grabs it a bit too harshly then adds, "Sorry . . . I . . ."

Karl stares at me. But instead of rage covering his eyes, he looks at me with a somber face and gently wipes the cassette tape with his fingers, and then places it in his front pocket.

"These flowers—I hope Nezzie woulda . . ."

Reaching out across the pain of twenty years, I touch his hand, "She would have loved them. And my mom, too."

He opens his mouth, but only air came out. We have nothing more to say. Except one thing.

"Karl, Rafe, there's one more thing. My name is Apple, and I don't give a rip if some people, some ignorant people," I emphasize looking at Rafe, "choose to see something ugly in it. One boy tried to take away my Indian half a long time ago by calling me a nasty name. But you know what? I am an apple. On the outside I may seem tough, but when broken there's a sweetness in my soul. I may not be Indian the way you are, or anyone else for that matter. But I am Indian. I'm a Turtle Mountain Ojibwe. And no one will ever take that away from me again."

Looking back as I step into the car, I watch as Karl then turns back to his son and cuffs him across the head. They return to the flower planting around the base of the sign, Nezzie's sign. And I also notice that there's no graffiti on it either. It's a small start, I guess. But Karl and his boy need to make sure they beautify their insides, too.

Chapter 31

THE REST OF THE drive to the airport is uneventful (read: no puking fests). We all agree a short vacation is just what this family could use before heading back to Minnesota. Time together is what we need — to heal, to rest. Actually, it's the destination that Judy has been haranguing us forever to visit — San Francisco, to be exact. California, here we come!

"Sssssan Francisssssco, here we come! I'll show you the ssssites of where I grew up!" Judy whistles . . . says (I'm trying sooo hard to be respectful of my elders, but, hey, it's a Work-in-Progress).

Baer has to sit next to me on the plane and keeps asking everyone around us for their puke bag. It's his new collection — vomit contraptions. Of course, my dad is amused by this because he thinks it means his son is following in his footsteps — a career in medicine. I say that it could also mean he has a future in garbage collection, but that didn't fly so well.

Our first few days in San Francisco are great. Judy shows us her row house on a crazy steep hill that she grew up in. Baer makes us all go to Madame Tussaud's Wax Museum. It's actually kind of kitschy. We walk around Fisherman's Wharf and take pictures of the sea lions sunning themselves on the docks. The tour of Alcatraz is awesome — especially after learning from Junior about the American

Indian takeover of the island in late 1969 to mid 1971 and occupied it as a rally call about the US government ignoring the needs of the Native population. See, I listen (sometimes). Seriously, read about it. In a way, I understand how those prisoners felt locked up in a tiny cell, only looking out at the world. But now I'm not hiding behind anything anymore. I feel a little freer.

On the last day we rent some bikes and ride along the San Francisco Bay. There's a park along the west end that's a picturesque spot for a picnic. Dad is a bit out of shape, so he practically collapses onto our blanket when we stop to eat. Judy, ever the tour guide, is explaining everything we can see.

"Now, kidssss, look out there. The fast moving currentssss are called the Golden Gate Straits. And if you look back towardssss the Wharf you can just make out Alcatraz. And there," she points, "iss the Golden Gate Bridge."

Baer, spitting chunks of his sandwich everywhere asks, "So what's on the other side of the bridge?"

"Well, let'ssss sssssee. It connectsss Sssssan Francissssco to Marin County. Without the bridge no one would be able to travel sssafely between the two to notice the beauty of both placesss."

My head jerks up at what Judy is saying. It's not just her sibilant s sounds calling birds everywhere, but I'm listening intently now, too.

"Before that bridge went up, people had to sssstay on their own sssside. It wasss too difficult to crosssss over, sssso people just gazed acrossss to a place they could never accessss."

O.M.G. That's it! That's it! I run over to Judy and kiss her on the cheek.

"Do you guys see?" I yell while pointing. "The Golden Gate is a *bridge*."

My family looks at me as if I'm crazy.

"That's what Little Nezzie was asking me the night before she died! Don't you remember me telling you about that? She asked me 'What's with the gold in gate?' Except what she was really asking was 'What's with the *Golden Gate*?'"

They're still not following. My dad feels my forehead, checking to see if I have a fever.

I'm on a roll though, "The Golden Gate . . . as in the *Bridge*!"

I have to catch them up with my whole Indian family gift of seeing hazy visions and asking questions of people to help to pinpoint the one area in life where they're not being true to themselves or can't see themselves.

"I guess Nezzie had this gift, too, then. She saw the one area in my life that I refused or couldn't see. And it was holding me back from being who I'm meant to be in life."

And I, again, point to the bridge.

Baer asks, "So, like, she meant you're as cold as steel?"

Sigh. Brothers, will they ever learn?

"No! See, the bridge? Like Judy said, it connects two separate worlds. I'm the bridge! Before I always felt like the ping pong ball where nobody wanted me on their side. Hovering between multiple worlds, never resting in any of them. I'll probably always feel that way, but it's who I'm meant to be. Get it? I am the one who needed to see both sides, especially my Native American side and the white side. It's the two sides of me, and like the Golden Gate Bridge, I don't ever really get to stay on either side, but get to travel everywhere in between."

My family just stares at me.

"And with my weird questions I have to ask? I think I needed to go across the bridge, and the multiple sites on the way, to see who I am meant to be, too."

Dad just looks at me and draws me into a bear hug. "Oh, Apple, your mother would have been so proud of you. We," he nods to Judy, "are so proud of you."

Turning to Judy and pointing above us, I ask, "Hey, Judes, what are those birds called flying around the Bay again?" Sorry, I had to do it.

"Ssssea gullssss, you sssssilly."

Wink. Wink. Birds beware.

Little Nezzie, I will never forget you. I will most likely always be in the middle. But there are good things in the middle: the center of a Twinkie, the middle of a Tootsie Pop, the jewel found in an oyster, the middle of a good book you never want to end, and the middle of an apology when you feel your heart melt with forgiveness.

Yep, I decide all things worthwhile are found in the middle. Which is why I've decided it's the only place for me — Apple in the Middle — to be.

Chapter 32

THE RETURN TO OUR home on Lake Minnetonka is uneventful (read: huge house, too quiet), and my return to the new school year is less than eventful (read: still nowhere to fit in).

Usually the first day of school takes me hours of morning prep to get ready. This year, however, I'm wearing my mom's boots and her jeans, a simple white top ($15.00 Kmart), and a smile. Grandma surprised me and packed my mom's things in my suitcase. It's almost like my mom's with me when I wear her clothes. But I know it's not really any tangible thing that's connecting me and my mother. It's so much more.

To my great joy (insert sarcasm) I have Mr. Markman again this year for eleventh-grade math. Apparently, he wanted to "move up with his students to continue their mathematical journey." I think he just wants to move to the classroom closer to the supply closet. Then he can be next to his drug of choice: whiteboard markers. Sniff sniff. But you didn't hear that from me.

So onward to my first class of the day: Introduction to Pre–calculus. Sounds like a barrel-o-fun.

Our first assignment of the day is to work with a partner and to try to figure out the review math problem Mr. Markman put on the board. Oh great. The ole' "find a partner" scenario. It's really deadly, if you ask me. The popular kids radiate towards one another, and the rest of us flounder about trying to make eye contact with the rejects hoping, praying that someone will work with us.

I can see Marcia Glasglow (queen of all two-fers) laughing and giggling at Steve Jernow (jock of ages). She's homing in on him big time. Already getting off the bus earlier today Marcia said, "Apple, oh my gosh, wha-at are you wearing? Like, I didn't know 'hoedown' was in again!" and she laughed all the way to home room. But I did see a coveting eye glance back at my boots.

She's priceless I tell ya. Yet for some reason, it just doesn't bother me as much today. And as I look at her the sensation comes bubbling up and I almost blurt out, "N 35?" Yep, you guessed it. Marcia has a slight gambling issue with online BINGO. So, when I asked her last year, "eye ate teen" and "before," it was *really* supposed to mean I-18 and B-4: BINGO call-outs.

Yet now I'm able to suppress my questions a bit. It's not time to help with her issue yet. Who knew I had an ounce of self-control? And BINGO was his name-O.

So back to math and Markman. I look around the room hoping for a partner and trying to make eye contact with nerdy Pete Smithers, the teenage mutant ninja Scrabble champ. Whenever you talk to him he adds up and calculates what your words would total on a Scrabble board game. Yep, I'm among winners here. (Count those words right there and that'd be thirty-two points.)

Except Mr. Markman says the unthinkable: "Boy and girls! Boys and girls. I've already paired you up. So, listen: Marcia and Pete will work together . . ."

Ha! The rest of the teacher's announcement fades out as I imagine those two working together. There is a God. And he is good.

"And Maria and Gabrielle will be partners; Jill, Kate, and Julie will work together; Michelle, Sonja and Liz will be a good group . . . hmmm, oh . . . let's see, and Apple and Steve will pair up."

What in the name of all that is Australian? Me and Mr. Steve Jernow? Mr. Football? Mr. Popular? Mr. I-have-the-most-perfect-face-if-you're-into-that-kind-of-thing Steve? He will be repulsed by having to be my partner.

Apple, get *ahold* of yourself. I see him pick up his notebook, and Marcia grabs his arm and says something inaudible. She laughs and he just shakes his head. She touches the top of her hair. Which reminds me that earlier this morning in the hallway she was blabbing how she just created a new hairstyle with her hair twisted up and knotted on her head. She called it the "messy bun." I called it the "mop on top" and said I've seen lots of people wear that. Firmly she retorted, "I invented it." Right, and I invented the Internet. (Oh, wait, that was Al Gore.)

I move my books to make room at the table for Steve to sit. His buddies all laugh as he sits down at my table, but he doesn't look in their direction. At least he gives me some dignity.

"OK, so I guess we'll just have to do this partner thing if we want a good grade."

"Yeah, I know, Apple" he quietly replies with a sideways glance.

Hmmm . . . I never noticed his eyes were two different colors. One ice blue and the other cerulean blue.

We both take out the assignment paper and decide our plan of attack. His buddies throw paper airplanes and spit-wads in our direction. I get it. This is killing him having to work with me.

He, being Steve Jernow, has no school supplies and asks to borrow a pencil. On the first day of school! Doesn't everyone love "Back to School" shopping? I'll have to update my chapter on "How Many Days Can a Football Player Not Bring Any School Supplies." This won't look good on his Ivy League applications.

"Apple! Are you listening?" he whispers.

"Oh, what? Umm, yeah, so for number two we need to use the distributive property formula."

"No, Apple," Steve says looking at me. Right at me. "Did you hear what I just said?"

"Well, I guess I was, umm, thinking about question number two . . ." I soooo wasn't listening.

He sighs and continues, "So I wanted to thank you for last year, like I was saying."

My face shoots up, "Thank me? For last year?"

"Yeah, if you were listening to me," he gives me a coy smile, "I was saying I wanted to thank you for last year. It was, well, it was sort of a tough year for us. For me and my family."

"Your family? Tough time?" *Steve, what could possibly have been tough in your perfect life?*

He just looks at me. Really looks at me. I wonder if I have a spitball in my hair. Maybe spinach between my teeth?

"Yeah, last year, see," he looks down at his feet. "Last year when my little brother was diagnosed with a rare congenital heart defect and well . . ."

"Oh, Steve, I never knew— "

Shaking his head (full thick blond hair with a few curls, if you like that sort of thing), he continues, "Umm, not too many people knew. Anyways, like I said, I wanted to thank you."

I must have the "deer-in-the-headlight" look because I have *NO* idea what in the world I would have done for him.

"Every day," he continues while I gather my jaw that had fallen to the floor, "well, most days, you were the only one who could make me laugh. Believe me, when my brother was going through his treatments, there was nothing funny about that and how it made him feel. But you, in class and in the lunchroom, always said something, well, hilarious. I'd watch you and Marcia face off and I have to say, you always beat her at her own game."

"But," I say confused, "I thought you and Marcia were, sort of, an item."

He chokes on his gum, "An item? With Miss Mop-on-Top? See," Steve winks, "I always listen to you. You're never afraid to say what's on your mind. Even if sometimes I have no idea what you mean."

Wow, he actually is impressed with my outbursts. He continues sharing about his little brother, Mitch, and how he lost his battle with heart disease this past June.

"No one knows what it's like to lose someone close to them. Not like this." Steve hangs his head in his hands for a few seconds.

I put my hand on his arm and whisper, "Oh, I actually know a little about that, too." And I ask him more about his brother, Mitch. And I also tell him about my best friend, Nezzie.

The bell is about to ring and I realize that Mr. Markman is collecting the math assignment that we're supposed to be doing.

"Steve, I'm so sorry, we should have done some of this worksheet. You would have been better off with another partner."

He laughs looking at me incredulously saying, "Didn't you know? I switched the partner names when Markman had his back turned. Markman didn't even notice. You know," and he makes an exaggerated sniffing gesture, "he sort of has other issues. I fixed it so I could work with you."

Is this my life? This is my life. My life in which I am no longer going to sit on the sidelines!

I'm feeling bold and brassy so I ask him right as the bell rings ending the class, "So, um, do you want to get some coffee, maybe Friday after school? I'd like to hear more about your brother." I can't believe I just asked out the school football star!

Steve looks at me, then over my shoulders to his buddies waiting for him in the doorway, "Oh, sorry. Can't."

Retreat! Retreat! Iceberg, right ahead! I put myself out there for the first time, and now my ship is sinking!

I'm just about to duck away, but Steve continues, "I can't Friday night 'cause it's my mom's birthday and I always take her for apple pie at our favorite place. But, how 'bout Saturday? I'd like to have you meet Mitch, maybe. I, umm, visit his grave every weekend. It'd be nice to have some company. It seems like you'd, well, understand."

Smile. Auntie Auber really did know what she's talking about. What did she say again? Grab the guy who knows his mom's birthday. And you know how I feel about mothers. Is he the pie to my apple? The yin to my yang? The BINGO card to the caller?

Chapter 33

THE NEXT FEW WEEKS of school are a blur. I won't lie to you: I don't suddenly get popular and I don't have a whirlwind romance with Mr. Perfect. Life just doesn't work that way. But I have a new sense of self, and the fact that Steve Jernow, hunk extraordinaire, likes my company gives a girl a lift.

I still have nowhere to sit in the lunchroom, except this time it doesn't seem so devastating. But I'm learning to just ask people if I can sit with them. I think everyone is just looking for friends. I don't need to be afraid to try to make friends or be afraid to be alone either. See, after this summer I now know that you can be in a crowd of people and still feel lonely and feel like an outcast. It's a full inner self, a complete soul that takes that solitude away. My grandparents both told me that in silence I'll hear better. In silence is equilibrium. It's hard for me to harness my mouth, but my time in the Turtle Mountains taught me that life is about overcoming our weaknesses and living in the quiet sometimes. 'Cause in silence, at times you speak the most eloquently.

Don't get me wrong people — every once in a while, I'll throw out a "G'day to ya', Govna!" just to keep things shakin'. And when I get those hazy visions and that crazy urge to ask a bizarre question to someone, I'm learning to hold back a bit. Grandma said I needed to rein it in and be gentler when I have a question to ask someone. I'm taking my role to help people more seriously.

Just 'cause I get that sudden vision in my mind and feel the urge to yell across the lunchroom, "Marcia, how much debt does your online BINGO account let you run up?" doesn't mean I should. See, it's all about personal growth.

One of my favorite new teachers this fall is Miss Phyllis. She's from out East and has a killer accent.

"Awwlright, class, tuday we'uh gonna write an essay." (Insert groans.) "It'll be abot ya' summa. *Anythin'* abot ya' summa is fine." Hmm, a new twist to the ever popular "What I Did Over My Summer Vacation." Is that allowed?

And so, I decide to write a version of my summer. But not about what I did, but who I met this summer. I met me. As I begin to write I realize that no paper is thick enough to support my heart's heavy burden. Feeling the pencil in my hand I know it will not be able to entirely etch the echoes of my summer.

> ***We Are All Connected***
> ***by Apple Starkington***
>
> We look for a purpose and a connection with each new family photo we study. Time with family forces us to look to the impossible idea of immortality through legacies, which bond us to those who went before us, and to those who will walk after us. Who, indeed, do I resemble? Whose likeness will I carry on?
>
> Gazing at my relatives around the table this summer, my thoughts turn inward as I question my ancestral connections. Looking into my eyes, what do my elders say? Whose legacy do I carry on? Who do I resemble?
>
> I have the eyes of my mother, my beautiful mother, who drinks in the quiet call of the Creator to return home.

My ears? From my grandfather, whose heart listened to Mother Nature as he gently gathered her bounty.

My nose? From my father, who covers the scent of human frailties with the healing balm of his medicine.

And my mouth? Inherited from all my ancestors, Grandmother, aunts, and all my relations whose sighs, laughter, tears, and tragedies still echo as they pass through my lips.

From where did I receive my heart? Every beat reverberates the echoing of the drum of those who walked before me as Native people succumbing to the trials and tribulations of their past.

And my soul? From those who prayed for me so many generations before.

You who feel lost, abandoned, steeped in solitude, remember: none of us is truly alone. None of us is truly abandoned.

Within us we carry all our relations from the Creator down to our little cousins. With every blink and breath we are encircled — body, mind, and spirit — to those who came before us and to those who loved us before we even know our own name, whatever it may be.

Gazing back to my family photographs from this summer, I pray that we all be blessed with eyes for peace, mouths for truth, and a heart for continuing our families' belief that through love, across the mile, and transcending the veil between this world and the next, we are all connected.

Take that, you teacher essay-lovin' cretins.

Epilogue

IT'S ONLY AFTER ONE has lived a long life that the creases of time can be smoothed out to truly see how certain incidents have affected your whole being. It was such a life fold the first summer I spent up in my beautiful Turtle Mountains. That summer, I learned the meaning of where I come from. But more importantly, I learned the meaning of who I am. And it doesn't mean one thing. We are made up of all those who have come before us and those who cross our paths: some good, some not so good.

There were many more Turtle Mountain summers that followed that first one. And there were many more times when I felt hopelessly lost in the middle of life, bouncing between the white world and the Native world and all the places in between that I'm still learning to understand. But I have my families — both of them — to guide me across the bridge, across the span of my days, aiding me so I can show others the value and views of all sides and to guide them in who they are meant to be.

Author's Note

FIRST TO MY FELLOW Native Americans, this book is intended to honor all that we are, and all that we are still intended to be. Our history, at times, has been a sad and tragic tale, one that has caused me to shed many tears and exhale countless sighs as I listened to stories and read the many books detailing our past. As it's said, one must learn about history—for if you do not, you will be condemned to repeat it. If you're not Native, I hope you research and search out more information from the many worthy texts on Native Americans. There are too many to list, but please, start reading. This is your history, too. Our Native history is the American story. I also encourage you to read books by Native people to learn their stories. Too many times other cultures try to write about Indian people. And they usually get it horribly wrong.

This book came out of the one thing that is ours, and ours alone: Native humor. It's our ability to maintain our humor—the joy and honor of life—and of dedication to family in the face of adversity that has helped us to carry on. Put those tears away, my friends, and as you read my book today remember that there is a time for sadness, but there is also a time for laughter. I hope you find a sense of joy reading this as you think back to your own family stories that keep you smiling still.

I began this book because of a beckoning voice I kept hearing: *Tell them the stories*. My first instinct was to push it away. How could I write a book? Who was I? But I felt this book was to be a legacy for my children to hear about my Turtle Mountain grandparents and what they taught me and are still teaching me today, even though their footprints are no longer on this Earth but in my soul. And like many Native people who are storytellers, I knew that the best way to share history and life lessons is through the telling of tales.

A few books and resources I suggest you read to learn more about the Turtle Mountain people are:

The History and Culture of the Turtle Mountain Band of Chippewa (Patricia Poitra and Karen Poitra); *History of the Turtle Mountain Band of Chippewa Indians* (Aun nish e naubay, Patrick Gourneau); information from the Turtle Mountain Chippewa Heritage Center in Belcourt, ND; *The Fur Trade in North Dakota* (edited by Virginia L. Heidenreich); Turtle Mountain Community College (Michif language resource book); and the *Turtle Mountain Band of Chippewa* website.

From these books and resources you will learn that the Turtle Mountain Band of Chippewa Indians (located in northern North Dakota) are members of the Pembina band. This band, or smaller group of a larger tribe, traveled across the Great Lakes to make their way into North Dakota. Many of these Native people intermarried with Cree Indians, Scottish people, other Ojibwe bands, and also French fur traders and trappers. The children of these couples became known as "Metis [may-tee]," a French term meaning mixed-blood, and their new language incorporated words and syntactic structure from the French, Cree, and Ojibwe. This combined, or creole language, is called the "Michif" language. Over time many Turtle Mountain people began simply referring to themselves as Michif.

Native American tribes, the Pembina band included, entered into many treaties with the United States government. And like all other tribes, the land that the Native people lived and took care of for generations was taken away with a signing of these documents. In 1863, more than one third of the state of North Dakota was Ojibwe land. What we have to remember is that in the beginning *all* of the United States was Indian land. Settlers at the time began to appeal to leaders in Washington, with the attitude of "Manifest Destiny," believing they had the right to Indian lands..

Many treaties were signed regarding North Dakota, but also everywhere in the United States. In one treaty, the US government acquired eleven million acres of land and then in turn gave it to white settlers to claim, to make their home on. Each acre was sold for eight cents. This was just one treaty of many for the Pembina band. Many more treaties would be signed over the years between various Minnesota and North Dakota Ojibwe bands. In these treaties across the United States, an area of land was "reserved"—the derivation of the word "Reservation"—for these Native people. So, Indian people never "gave up" their land. Again, I ask that you read how your own local area's land was once Indian country and see what the history is. Where your house, school, and everywhere is located today was once Indian lands.

These stories in *Apple in the Middle*—some from my own life, and some things I've been fortunate enough to learn from other Native people—are a way to pass on my Native American heritage, culture, and history. Some readers may ask what "statement" I am trying to make with this book. No statement; I'm simply telling a story. Portraying the Michif language was, at times, difficult to decide upon, as the correct spellings vary from regions and even between families. I've tried throughout the book to let you into what my eyes have seen, what my ears have heard, and most importantly, what my heart has felt.

All mistakes are mine, and mine alone.

* * *

Thank you to NDSU Press editor in chief, Suzzanne Kelley, for loving *Apple* first. You, along with my peer reviewers and staff at the press, have made this a much better story.

Again, thank you to my parents for allowing me to see your own love of reading and stories. You gave this little nut a place to plant roots and to grow while always keeping my feet firmly planted in family.

To my childhood friends, Jean and Jennifer, thank you for helping to instill my quirky and offbeat sense of humor, which added laughter to our sometimes dull 1980s lives. Speaking of the '80s, a shout out to Michelle, Sonja, Liz . . . and the Loyola gang (whose names *may* have found their way into my book): my life is so much fuller because of all of you. And, shhh, to all of our youthful shenanigans . . . but such fun! Of course, my Gopher friends: Jill, Kate, and Julie (and the rest)! I think I learned more from our time together than any university class. Who knew college could be so entertaining?

To all my former teaching spots — colleagues and students — you made my work always interesting and filled my mind with stories (and with nightmares sometimes, but that's another book).

Amanda B., I owe you so much for reading my very rough first draft! Thank you!

To my sister, Anne, and brother, Mike, aunties, uncles, cousins, nieces, nephews, and extended family: you have paved the way for me in every aspect. Many hugs and praise to you as family, parents, siblings, and friends. Sending love to my grandparents in the next life. Keep looking out for us.

To the many Marys in my life: what would I do without you all?

Miigwech to all of my Native American friends, colleagues, professors, and students. Even though you may not know it, only with your guidance was this book possible. And chi miigwech to Mike H. for inviting me into leadership possibilities I never dreamed I could do.

To the PhD professors and fellow students at the University of Minnesota: I appreciate all of you as you seek to uncover a better world for education.

St. Catherine University faculty, staff, and students: What a wonderful and welcoming place to work. My praise and thanksgiving to you all.

Thanks to all of you I haven't had the chance to name. There are so many of you to acknowledge, and I do so in my thoughts each day.

Finally, to my husband and two girls: this story begins with you. Thank you for allowing me to sit at my computer way too many times when you were around (and for feeding you a multitude of frozen pizzas while I worked on my book). Your support and ideas have been instrumental in this manuscript. I love you all more than you can imagine.

* * *

The poem, "We Are All Connected," which appears at the front of this book, is written by Dawn Quigley. This poem has appeared in somewhat different forms in *Native American Times* and *Yellow Medicine Review: A Journal of Literature, Art and Thought*. The author retains copyrights to this poem in all versions.

Appendix: Recipes

APPLE'S FAVORITE FOOD

Every family has their own recipes, but these are the ones I've watched my cousins, Auntie, and Grandma make. I have changed a few things to make them easier—and hey, easier is always a good thing. Remember, like Mooshum says, "You gotta eeeeat!" And Kookum reminds us to always read the entire recipe before you even start. Be sure to work with an adult with the baeng, because you're frying in oil and it can get extremely hot. Thanks to my auntie for writing this first recipe down for me!

BAENG, OR BANG

(Turtle Mountain Indian Fry bread recipe from my Auntie Charlene Pays)

2 T yeast
½ T sugar
¼ cup warm water

Put in a small bowl by itself.
Cover the bowl with towel. Set aside.

4 cups flour
¼ t salt
¼ cup sugar
2 eggs
1 cup hot water (divided)
⅓ cup vegetable oil

Mix the first three ingredients. Set aside in a bowl with a towel over it.

Mix 2 cups of the flour, the salt, and the sugar in a large bowl. Add the eggs, oil, and ½ cup of the warm water. Mix. Add the remaining 2 cups of flour and water to make dough. Add the yeast mixture. (You may need to add a bit more flour or water.) Dough will be sticky.

Turn out dough onto a clean surface. Knead until it is not sticky (about 1 ½ minutes). Place dough in clean, greased bowl with a clean towel over it and let the dough rise until about double in size (about 60 minutes).

Now, you get to punch the dough down (gently) and place it on a clean surface. Place a clean towel over the dough so it doesn't dry out as you are frying.

Meanwhile, in a sturdy Dutch oven (big tall pot) on low medium heat, heat 2 inches of vegetable oil to medium heat (be sure you're doing this with a parent!).

Now, put the dough on the counter right next to the stove. When the hot oil sizzles after you put a tiny bit of dough in it and it floats to the top, you're ready to make baeng!

Uncover a corner of the dough and pat down on a little piece (about ¼ to ⅓ inch thick). Use a sharp knife and cut the flattened dough into a triangle-type shape and slice a 1 to 2 inch slit into the center. Hold it up and pull it a bit. Be sure to keep the rest of the dough ball covered, or it will dry out.

Using long-handled tongs, gently add the triangle-ish dough into the hot oil. Let it cook until the edges become copper brown. Turn it carefully so you don't splatter oil. When the second side is also copper brown, lift it out and set it on a cookie sheet lined (on counter right next to stove) with paper towels. Let cool, then eat until you get full. Repeat.

**hints:* You may only want to put 3 baeng in the pot at once so they don't get over crowded. Make sure the insides are cooked, which is why you smush the dough gently before you put it in the oil. It'll take you a few times to perfect it, but you can do it! This makes about 22 baeng.

Every family has its own bullet recipe, but here is one to try.

BULLETS

(Turtle Mountain meatball in broth from my cousin Shelby [Bauer] Vega)

1 lb ground beef
a handful of saltine crackers (crunched down into crumbs)
Salt and pepper to taste
¼ cup finely chopped onions
3 to 4 T flour
6 to 8 cups of water (some people use only water, but I like a bit of broth in mine, so you can also use water and a few beef bouillon cubes)
*optional: cut up potatoes

Gently mix the first 4 ingredients. Shape them into golf ball sized meatballs. Sprinkle the flour onto a plate and roll the meatballs in the flour. Put water in a pot on the stove to boil. Put the bullets into the soup pot on the stove and gently boil. If you add potatoes, add them to the water now, too.

Boil on low to medium heat for 20 minutes. Eat! And repeat!

GALLETTE

(Turtle Mountain biscuit-like bread from my chef cousin, Anthony Bauer)

- 4 cups of flour
- 2 cups of 1% milk
- ¼ cup vegetable oil
- 1 tsp salt
- ¼ cup sugar
- 5 tsp baking powder

Mix dry ingredients with whisk. Make well in the center and add ¼ cup oil. Heat milk till warm, add in center also and mix with your hands folding flour in. (You may need to add up to ½ cup more flour until dough is not sticky). Flatten dough and put on greased cookie sheet. Poke holes on top randomly. Bake in 400 degree oven for 20 minutes. You may need to flip and bake an additional 5 minutes. (May take a few minutes longer depending on oven). Let stand for 15 minutes before cutting, or wrap in plastic wrap and refrigerate. Eat!

Gigawabamin, my friends!

Glossary

Anishinaabe (*ä-ni-shi-' nȯ -bā*) noun

1. Ojibwe for: "original people" (i.e., what they call themselves in their native language). This name, Anishinaabe, is a more accurate term of the Ojibwe people. There is confusion in the non–Native world as many ask: *Who is a Chippewa person? Who is Ojibwe?* Both of these terms are actually a misunderstood translation from early interaction with the tribes. The term "Ojibwe" may have come from a description of the puckering in seams of moccasins worn by the Anishinaabe. And Chippewa is even more of a misinterpretation. If you say "Ojibwe" slowly, you can see how it could sound like "Chippewa."

   Many times, a tribal name is used because of language in a historical treaty (for example: The Turtle Mountain Band of Chippewa Indians). It is always best to ask Native people what tribal nation they are from, or how they identify themselves.

baeng (*bang*) noun ("bang" is a more common spelling)

1. French for: Native American fry bread (bread dough, made with yeast or baking powder, which is fried in oil, instead of baked). During the early days when Native people were forced onto reservations, they received food items from the US government that were a part of the treaty agreement. Being ever the resourceful and creative people they were and still are, Native Americans used flour, yeast, and oil from these government payments to make fry bread, taking simple ingredients and turning them into a delicacy. Talk about making lemonade out of lemons.

bullets (*bul-ets*) noun

1. French for: meatballs made in a soup, usually made for New Year's Day. Relatives would go house to house visiting each other on that day, wishing everyone "La bonne année!" Happy New Year!

eh bien (*eh-**bah*** [But make sure to really stretch out the second syllable for full Turtle Mountain affect, and dip your inflection at the end.]) exclamatory phrase

1. French for: Oh well, or For Pete's sake! (as in "Eh bien, don't tell me you can't do that math problem.") Remember that the Michif language from the Turtle Mountains had many French words mixed in, and therefore make sure you use the nasal pronunciation when you say it. It's sort of like shoving the words up your throat and having it come out your nose.

eya (*e-**yeuh***) noun

1. Ojibwe for: yes (as in "Do you want more baeng?" "Eya!") The Michif language spoken in the Turtle Mountains is a mixture of French, Cree, and Ojibwe. These various languages make up a creole, or mixture, and create an entire new language.

gigawabamin (*gi-guh-wa-bu-min*) interjection

1. Ojibwe for: a type of farewell, see you again. There is no word for the exact match of "goodbye" in the Ojibwe language as we are all related and will always meet someone again, either in this world or the next. Being Indian means "never having to say goodbye."

gallette (*gul-et*) noun

1. French for: Native American baking powder biscuit (not cut out individually, but usually made in a pan or on a cookie sheet.) Have you noticed that there's a *lot* of food in our Native culture? Eya!

kookum (***ku**-kum*) noun

1. Cree and Michif for: grandmother. Grandmothers, and all elders in general, are revered and honored in Native American culture. Elders are to be given respect, as they have lived a long life and learned many lessons, so be sure to listen to them. And they can cook, so learn from them, because the best way to pass on your culture is to learn the food your ancestors made.

mooshum (***mu**-shum*) noun

1. Cree and Michif for: grandfather. Grandfathers, as with all elders, deserve respect and honor. So, make sure you jump up and give them the best chair in the house next time you see them. Many times, a grandfather won't tell you how to live, but you must watch and learn. Listen to his stories because years from now, you'll reflect back and yearn for his wisdom.

le blanc (*lu-**blon***) noun

1. Michif for: white person. A translation could be "white."

About the Author

Dawn Quigley, enrolled member of the Turtle Mountain Band of Ojibwe, North Dakota, is an assistant professor in the Education Department at St. Catherine University (St. Paul, Minnesota). She completed her PhD at the University of Minnesota in 2018. Her website, nativereadermn.blogspot.com, offers support for educators in finding, evaluating, and implementing Native American curriculum content from an indigenous perspective. In addition to her coming-of-age Young Adult novel, *Apple in the Middle*, Dawn has more than twenty-five published articles and poems in mainstream magazines, academic journals, and newspapers, including *American Indian Quarterly, Yellow Medicine Review: A Journal of Indigenous Literature, Art and Thought, Indian Country Today, Hollywood and Vine* magazine, and the *Minneapolis Star Tribune*.

Dawn was awarded the St. Catherine University Denny Prize Award for Distinction in Writing and has been a finalist in both the Minnesota Loft Literary Center's MN Emerging Writer award and its Mentor Series.

She lives in the metro area in Minnesota with her husband and two girls.

About the Press

North Dakota State University Press (NDSU Press) exists to stimulate and coordinate interdisciplinary regional scholarship. These regions include the Red River Valley, the state of North Dakota, the plains of North America (comprising both the Great Plains of the United States and the prairies of Canada), and comparable regions of other continents. We publish peer reviewed regional scholarship shaped by national and international events and comparative studies.

Neither topic nor discipline limits the scope of NDSU Press publications. We consider manuscripts in any field of learning. We define our scope, however, by a regional focus in accord with the press's mission. Generally, works published by NDSU Press address regional life directly, as the subject of study. Such works contribute to scholarly knowledge of region (that is, discovery of new knowledge) or to public consciousness of region (that is, dissemination of information, or interpretation of regional experience). Where regions abroad are treated, either for comparison or because of ties to those North American regions of primary concern to the press, the linkages are made plain. For nearly three-quarters of a century, NDSU Press has published substantial trade books, but the line of publications is not limited to that genre. We also publish textbooks (at any level), reference books, anthologies, reprints, papers, proceedings, and monographs. The press also considers works of poetry or fiction, provided they are established regional classics or they promise to assume landmark or reference status for the region. We select biographical or autobiographical works carefully for their prospective contribution to regional knowledge and culture. All publications, in whatever genre, are of such quality and substance as to embellish the imprint of NDSU Press.

We changed our imprint to North Dakota State University Press in January 2016. Prior to that, and since 1950, we published as the North Dakota Institute for Regional Studies Press. We continue to operate under the umbrella of the North Dakota Institute for Regional Studies, located at North Dakota State University.

Apple in the Middle is the first volume in the NDSU Press Contemporary Voice of Indigenous Peoples Series.